A DEADLY HABIT

Simon Brett

CRÈME de la CRIME

This first world edition published 2018
in Great Britain and the USA by
Crème de la Crime, an imprint of
SEVERN HOUSE PUBLISHERS LTD of
Eardley House, 4 Uxbridge Street, London W8 7SY
Trade paperback edition first published
in Great Britain and the USA 2019 by
SEVERN HOUSE PUBLISHERS LTD

British Library Cataloguing in Publication Data
A CIP catalogue record for this title is available from the British Library.

ISBN-13: 978-1-78029-105-5 (cased)
ISBN-13: 978-1-84751-921-4 (trade paper)
ISBN-13: 978-1-78010-977-0 (e-book)

This is a work of fiction. Names, characters, places and incidents
are either the product of the author's imagination or are used fictitiously.
Except where actual historical events and characters are being described
for the storyline of this novel, all situations in this publication are
fictitious and any resemblance to actual persons, living or dead,
business establishments, events or locales is purely coincidental.

All Severn House titles are printed on acid-free paper.

Severn House Publishers support the Forest Stewardship Council™ [FSC™],
the leading international forest certification organisation.
All our titles that are printed on FSC certified paper carry the FSC logo.

Typeset by Palimpsest Book Production Ltd.,
Falkirk, Stirlingshire, Scotland.
Printed and bound in Great Britain by
TJ International, Padstow, Cornwall.

A DEADLY HABIT

To
The People Who Care

'There was always whisky – the medicine against despair.'

Graham Greene, *The Human Factor*

ONE

'There is one condition,' said Frances.

'Oh?' asked Charles Paris, feigning both ignorance and innocence.

'You'll have to give up drinking.'

'Ah.' He had known it would be that. In Frances's view, it was his drinking that had broken up their marriage. Charles saw things slightly differently. He thought the stresses of his chosen profession, the long separations inevitable in an actor's life, bore at least as much responsibility as alcohol. The fact that the long separations had made him particularly susceptible to the charms of young actresses hadn't helped either.

But he wasn't about to offer up that extenuation. He had been over the same ground too often with Frances, and he had not in the past found it fruitful territory. For a start, raising the subject was an unnecessary reminder of his infidelities. And discussions on such matters tended to end up with her asserting that drink had always contributed to the erosion of his willpower, which allowed him to succumb to the blandishments of other women. Marital arguments, he knew, were always circular rather than linear.

And in this particular argument, he was aware how high the stakes were. His wife had offered him a lifeline. It would be folly not to take hold of it.

Although Charles and Frances had never divorced, it had been a long time since they had lived together as man and wife. He had ceased to be a permanent resident in the family home when their daughter Juliet had been comparatively young. There had been rapprochements and reconciliations, but none had lasted more than a few weeks. And now Frances was offering the possibility of their resuming cohabitation.

It was Charles's view that they had never stopped loving each other. This was another aspect of their relationship which his wife might have seen slightly differently. She had a more practical perception of love than he did. For him it was just a warm emotional feeling; for her it involved certain duties and responsibilities.

'Suppose,' he suggested, 'I were to cut down on my drinking . . .?'

His tone was tentative, and Frances's reaction demonstrated that it had every right to be tentative. 'You've tried that many times, and it's never worked. You know as well as I do that you're incapable of saying, "Just the one" and meaning it. Or perhaps you do mean it when you say the words, but the minute you're offered a second drink, all that resolution melts away. You don't have the self-control to cut down.'

'Oh,' he said facetiously, 'are you saying I should be standing up in an Alcoholics Anonymous meeting and announcing: "I'm Charles and I'm an alcoholic"?'

Frances looked straight at him. Unavoidable eye contact.

'Yes,' she said.

They had had conversations on this subject, many times, but Frances had never before been so direct. She had blamed many of his short-comings as a husband on his drinking, without actually branding him an alcoholic. To hear that that was what she really thought came as quite a shock.

Charles's own view was that, yes, he did like a drink, and he often drank more than he should. Certainly more than was recommended by the mealy-mouthed government advisors on such matters. But he was never out of control.

Alcoholics, on the other hand, were people who lost control, who lost jobs, who lost families, who ended up in the gutter. He'd never been that bad.

But, even if Frances had slightly overstated the case, he still had to take what she said seriously. Their marriage was at a pivotal stage. She was talking of retiring from being headmistress of a girls' school, and had received a windfall of more money than she was expecting from her mother's will. This encouraged the idea of her moving out of her relatively small flat in Finchley into a larger one. During the summer holidays, she began looking for something suit-able. She'd seen a property she liked in Highgate, and had started the tortuous process, more complicated in England than in any other country in the world, of house purchase.

This had coincided with the rapprochement between Frances and her husband. They'd started to see more of each other on a regular basis. Some nights Charles had not returned to his studio flat in Hereford Road. They had even, on a few occasions, shared a bed, and indulged in the leisurely delights of geriatric sex.

Charles would never have dared to raise the subject himself, but to his surprise Frances, in a languorous post-coital moment, had raised the possibility of their cohabiting in the new flat. New flat, new start. As she tactlessly reminded him, neither of them was getting any younger. She would soon be retired and he . . . well . . .

It is always difficult to define the moment when an actor retires. In a profession of such uncertainty, every job one takes could be the last. Telephone silence from one's agent is not unusual, particularly if one's agent is named Maurice Skellern. Charles had become inured, over the years, to months without communication from Maurice. And to hearing, when his agent finally did ring, about the wonderfully lucrative deal he'd just negotiated for one of his more eminent clients. Charles kept saying he should break up with Maurice and get a more dynamic agent, but, as with many things in his life, he never got round to doing anything about it.

Some actors do make public announcements of their retirement from 'the business' but, sadly, unless they're very big names, it is rare that anyone notices. Anyway, unless suffering total medical breakdown, hope still springs eternal in the thespian breast. Even an actor on his deathbed does not discount the possibility of a call from the National Theatre, asking him to give his Lear. And if such a call were to come, the invalid would immediately leap up and start learning the lines. What is known by actors as 'Doctor Theatre' has achieved many Lazarus-like risings from the dead.

Charles Paris didn't plan to retire. He hoped the ending of his life as an actor would be coterminous with his death. But he knew he had little control over either eventuality.

Meanwhile, as he had done for most of his career, he spent a great deal more time out of work than in. But, though he would never admit it to a soul, he still nursed a secret ambition that one day the Really Big Break would come. He was, after all, only in his late fifties. Show business provided many examples of people whose careers had gone stratospheric at considerably greater ages.

Anyway, at the time that Frances was going through the horrendous process of house-hunting, Charles Paris actually had some work. In the West End, no less. With a contract that guaranteed an income for the next four months. The four-week rehearsal period was due to start in late August, and the play's last night would be at the end of November. That kind of security was almost unprecedented in his career.

He remembered the call he'd received from Maurice Skellern which first mentioned the job.

'All right, who is it?' Charles had asked, the moment the caller identified himself.

'What do you mean – "Who is it?" It's Maurice. Your agent. You know it's me.'

'No, I meant which of your other clients is it, whose wonderful new job you want to crow to me about?'

'Now, Charles, that's very unfair.' The voice was aggrieved and reproachful. 'Here I am, working away tirelessly on your behalf, and what thanks do I get?'

'Maurice, you haven't rung me for more than four months.'

'That doesn't mean I haven't been working for you. Some agents, I know, are sprinters. But you have to think of me more as a marathon man. I deal in long-term strategy for my clients. I'm not in the business for the quick bucks.'

'I wouldn't mind a few quick bucks every now and then,' said Charles wistfully. 'Or even some slow ones. Bucks of any kind'd do.'

'Don't come the "hearts and flowers" routine with me,' Maurice snapped. 'You know it's never going to work. I think you're very ungrateful, given the way I'm continually putting myself on the line for you.'

'And which particular line is it you put yourself on for me?'

'Charles, you're being cynical and unhelpful. I've half a mind to ring off and not tell you about the wonderful job I've engineered for you.'

'For *me*? Sorry, could you repeat that? I thought I heard you say you had engineered a job *for me.*'

'That's exactly what I said, Charles. And I think it shows that my "softly, softly" approach is paying off. I know there are agents who keep on putting their clients up for every job that comes along—'

'Being put up for the occasional one wouldn't hurt.'

'I'm not listening to you, Charles,' Maurice continued imperturbably. 'I will continue saying what I was saying. I believe in ignoring all casting opportunities which are not suitable for my clients. But when the right part comes up . . . I strike like a cobra!'

Charles didn't let himself get sidetracked by the incongruous image of the Savile Row-suited Maurice Skellern striking like a cobra. 'Are you saying the right part for me has come up?'

'I most certainly am. It could have been written for you.'

Charles Paris's mind instantly filled with thoughts of Hamlet, Henry V, and 'the complex central character in a new play by one of our brightest new theatrical talents', as he asked, 'What is the part?'

'It's a monk.'

'A monk?' This was not initially promising. Charles recognized that there were many parts which might reflect aspects of his own character, but monks weren't on the list. On the other hand, there were monks who'd done more with their lives than go to endless repetitive services and illuminate manuscripts. Rasputin, for example. He was a monk who did quite a lot more with his life. He had a lot of sex, for a start. Yes, Charles Paris could see himself taking the leading role in a ground-breaking new work about the life of Rasputin.

'What's the play?' he asked.

'New one.' Promising. 'Called *The Habit of Faith*. Written by someone called Seamus Milligan.'

'Name doesn't mean anything to me.'

'Nor to me. Apparently, he's been around for a long time, though. But the exciting thing about the whole project . . .'

While Maurice theatrically held the pause, Charles conjectured what was about to come. Obviously, confirmation that he was being asked to interview for the leading role.

'. . . is,' Maurice continued, 'that the leading role is being played by Justin Grover.'

'Ah.'

Charles knew the name. Almost everyone in the country, if not in the entire world, knew the name.

The two had long ago played Rosencrantz and Guildenstern in a production of *Hamlet* at the Imperial Theatre, Bridport. ('In many productions of the play it is hard to tell the two characters apart. That wasn't a problem last night. Justin Grover's acting was so subtle as to be virtually invisible, whereas Charles Paris overacted shamelessly.' *Bridport Herald*.)

The two were not natural soulmates, but had rubbed along all right, as most people do in theatrical companies. The job is not forever, and backstage harmony is preferable to open conflict.

Charles's recollections of the production were now a bit hazy. He remembered there had been a very pretty young girl playing Ophelia. He – and most of the rest of the company – fancied her rotten. What was her name? Oh God, he really was finding it ever harder to remember names. Wasn't that an early sign of Alzheimer's, he thought gloomily. Anyway, he knew he hadn't made any moves on the young Ophelia. Chiefly because he was involved in a rather steamy and short-lived affair with Gertrude. Oh no, he couldn't remember her name either.

The Gertrude was married, so any action between them tended to happen inside the Imperial Theatre. They got to know the structure of Shakespeare's play very well, and took advantage of the times when neither Gertrude nor Rosencrantz (or was it Guildenstern?) were required on stage.

As a result, Charles spent less time than he might have done in the dressing room he shared with Justin Grover. Which was perhaps a blessing, because there were one or two little things about his fellow actor that annoyed Charles. And a shared dressing room is the kind of crucible in which little niggles can, given enough time, develop into extreme annoyances.

Charles was by nature a tolerant soul. He knew that everyone found their own way of dealing with the nervous challenge of going onstage every night. But he did draw the line at Buddhist chanting.

He wouldn't have minded if he thought Justin Grover was getting a positive benefit from his pre-show routine. Or if he thought his fellow actor's Buddhist beliefs were more than ankle-deep. But he couldn't help feeling that the whole thing was just a fad, another means by which Justin Grover could draw attention to himself. In spite of spending his entire life working in the theatre, Charles Paris still had a very English, visceral dislike of anything that came under the heading of 'showing off'.

Also, he wasn't convinced that Justin was that good an actor. Far too technical for Charles's taste. Every move, every intonation, every hand gesture was practised in private until it met its executor's satisfaction. Justin Grover was always acting in his own play, which was slightly different from the one that the rest of the company were in. This approach was not calculated to make him popular in a theatrical ensemble.

But, of course, once he became famous, once he was playing leading parts, it worked wonderfully for him. Rather than him trying to fit in with the rest of the cast, the whole production would be constructed around his studied mannerisms.

So how was it that Justin Grover began to get leading parts? It was a conundrum over which Charles had frequently puzzled, together with the automatically accompanying question: And how was it that Charles Paris didn't begin to get leading parts?

He knew that luck played a huge part in an actor's success, but luck alone could not explain the scale of Justin Grover's domination of the theatrical world.

Success in America had been the key. Justin had the kind of agent – as unlike Maurice Skellern as it was possible to be – whose ambitions for his clients spanned the Atlantic. He had engineered some small parts in US miniseries for Justin. The small parts led to bigger parts, and the raising of his international profile had led to his being more valued in the UK. As a recognizable face from American imports, he began to get bigger parts on British television. As a recognizable face from British television, offers started to come in for bigger stage parts. Since most British theatre-goers spent most of their time sitting in front of televisions, the name on a theatre poster of someone from *Coronation Street* or *EastEnders* stood a better chance of bringing in the punters. This was something of which producers of touring theatre were well aware, and Justin Grover spent a couple of years going round the country in quite juicy and lucrative parts, raising his face recognition in venues as far apart as Weston-Super-Mare and Milton Keynes.

But again, it was America which raised him from that level to West End stardom. *Vandals and Visigoths* was not the first computer game that Hollywood's poverty of imagination had turned into a feature film, but it was one of the few which really caught on with the cinema-going public. In the first movie there was some vague fidelity to historical facts about the Germanic tribes who hastened the fall of the Roman Empire, but even in that one there were sorcerers, shape-shifters and dragons, as well as the requisite bloodshed and nudity.

For the second and subsequent films in the franchise, in the fine tradition of Hollywood, historical accuracy was thrown out of the window. The influence of magic, in the post-*Harry Potter* boom, intensified. The incidence of bloodshed and nudity increased. Every episode saw more of the original characters killed off.

And greater amounts of the screen-time were filled with computer-generated monsters. Of these, by far the most popular was the Skelegator. As its name implied, this was a kind of skeletal alligator, coloured, for no particular reason, a luminescent green. But the creature had skills not possessed by your standard alligator. Though its main means of destruction remained its rows of razor-sharp teeth, a Skelegator had the ability to stand on its back legs and wield a variety of swords, daggers, maces and axes in its prehensile hands. Merchandising of Skelegators really caught on. Few households with children in them lacked a set of luminescent green figurines. Mugs, toothbrushes, school bags, pyjamas and duvet covers all featured the odious reptiles. And no children's fancy-dress party went by without the appearance of at least two Skelegators.

As the movie franchise developed, the number of Skelegators – and their role in the proceedings – increased. Soon they had a leader, double the size of his acolytes, called Spurg. He represented pure evil, and his mission in life was to destroy as many Vandals and Visigoths as he could, in as bloody a way as possible.

But, riding above all the carnage, impervious to the surrounding slaughter, equal to any dastardly challenge that Spurg might throw at him, rose the figure of the Visigoth leader, Sigismund the Strong. And the actor who played that part was called Justin Grover.

From the moment he landed the role, his international profile just grew and grew. The success of the movies fed the sales of the original *Vandals and Visigoths* computer game. The sales of the computer game sent more people all over the world scurrying to the cinemas or downloading the movies on to whatever was the latest technology.

Justin Grover had ceased to be an actor; he had become a brand. The image of Sigismund the Strong's head in its horned helmet (totally wrong period for either a Visigoth or a Vandal) became almost as recognizable as that of Sherlock Holmes, Mickey Mouse or Elvis Presley. Figurines of Sigismund the Strong outsold even those of Spurg the Skelegator.

The result was that there was no media outlet where Justin Grover was not visible. Charles Paris got sick of reading articles where the former Guildenstern pontificated about how seriously he took his art as an actor, what lengths he went to in order to inhabit the persona of Sigismund the Strong. And how his real love would always be for the theatre.

Which, Charles reckoned, if you were making squillions of pounds from your screen career, was an easy thing to say.

He wondered if, on the sets of the *Vandals and Visigoths* films, no action could take place until their star had finished his Buddhist chanting.

Justin Grover had been awarded an OBE 'for services to the theatre', and in showbiz circles it was reckoned to be only a matter of time before the knighthood came along.

As a result of this worldwide fame, of course, he now had *carte blanche* to do whatever theatre he chose to. His name would put bums on seats, and no theatre producer was too worried that many of those bums would be dressed up as Vandals, Visigoths or Skelegators, who might be disappointed if he didn't wear his horned helmet as Hamlet.

So, whenever a gap in the *Vandals and Visigoths* shooting schedule allowed, Justin Grover would do a short run in a West End theatre, taking the lead role in whatever play he fancied.

Which was how it came about that he was doing *The Habit of Faith.*

'What?' Charles asked Maurice Skellern on the phone when the name of the play was first mentioned. 'And you've arranged for me to be interviewed for a part in it?'

'In a manner of speaking, yes.'

Charles had heard too many of his agent's 'manners of speaking' not to be suspicious. 'What exactly do you mean?'

'I had a call from the producer's office checking your availability for the run.'

'And is that why you're ringing me now? To ask if I'm available.'

'No, of course not, Charles.' Maurice chuckled at the idea. 'I said you were. You're always available.'

Charles decided not to contest the insult. 'So, are you ringing to let me know when they want to do an interview?'

'No, there's no interview involved. They're offering you the part. West End. Three months guaranteed.'

'They're *offering* me the part?' Charles echoed, dumbstruck.

'Yes.'

'Why?'

'Apparently, Justin Grover remembered working with you in the past and thought he might do you a good turn.'

Charles's reaction was divided into two parts. Half of it was: 'Patronizing bugger! If he thinks I'm going to accept charity from him . . .' The other half was: 'On the other hand, three months guaranteed on West End money . . .'

He didn't vocalize either to Maurice. Instead, he said coolly, 'Well, get them to send me a script—'

'Oh, we don't need to bother with that. I've said you'll do it.'

'What! Maurice, as my agent, it is your job to—'

'Well, you will do it, won't you?'

There was a silence before Charles conceded, 'Probably, yes.'

'See, I knew you would. Why bother farting around with sending scripts, eh?'

Charles Paris's next words were every actor's instinctive question. 'What's the money?'

Maurice told him. It sounded a gratifyingly large amount, but Charles still said, 'Have you tried getting them up a bit?'

'It's good money, Charles. And we don't want to make waves. Don't want the producers changing their minds, do we?'

'Well,' said Charles, 'give me overnight to think about it.'

'No time for that. I've already said you'll accept.'

'But, Maurice—'

'Come on, this is the best offer you've had for a long time, Charles.'

'Maybe . . .'

'The *only* offer you've had for a long time.'

'All right. There's no need to rub it in.'

There was a silence before Maurice asked, 'Well, aren't you going to say something?'

'Like what?'

'Like "thank you".'

'Maurice, can I get this right?'

'Get what right?'

'Justin Grover decided he wanted me to play a part in *The Habit of Faith* . . .?'

'Ye-es,' the agent conceded cautiously.

'He told the producers that, and asked them to offer me the part . . .?'

'Right . . .'

'And they then rang you and offered it?'

'OK . . .'

'And you're asking me to say, "thank you"?'

'Of course. It's only polite.'

'But can you tell me what I'm meant to be thanking you for? What contribution did you actually make to my getting this part in *The Habit of Faith*?'

'I was at the end of the phone when they called about it,' said an aggrieved Maurice Skellern.

TWO

A few days later, at his studio flat in Hereford Road, Charles did receive a copy of the play script. After nipping to the café round the corner to pick up a large strong Americano, he settled into his armchair to read it.

Long habit made him look at the cast list first. It was headed by the name of Abbot Ambrose, the part, some instinct told him, that Justin Grover would be playing. Then there were a lot of characters called Brother This and Brother That. The accompanying letter from the production office announced that Charles Paris would be playing the part of Brother Benedict.

There was only one female character in the *dramatis personae*, a fact which gave him a knee-jerk reaction of disappointment. It wasn't that he was living in hope of starting an affair with some nubile cast member. Given the improving state of his relationship with Frances, he was way beyond such fantasies (well, that is to say, unless the right opportunity presented itself). His disappointment arose, he told himself, from the fact that he found exclusively masculine company rather stifling. The presence of women in a production always provided some necessary leavening.

Still, on the plus side, there was a strong chance some of the backstage staff might be female. And members of the stage management had provided some of the most rewarding interludes in the life of Charles Paris.

He was also a little put off by the fact that the only female in the cast list was called 'The Girl'. Experience had taught him that plays featuring characters with names like 'The Man', 'The Woman' or, even worse, 'He' and 'She', had a strong tendency to be pretentious.

He read through *The Habit of Faith*. Like all plays set in monasteries, the *dramatis personae* were fairly predictable. There was the Abbot, a Saintly Man Whose Moral Integrity Was Hard Won And Whose Continuing Internal Conflict Between Warring Aspects Of His Personality Was Expressed In A Lot Of Long Monologues.

Then, inevitably, there was The Monk Who Had Lost His Faith, The Monk Who Had Difficulty Controlling His Lust Towards Women,

The Monk Who Had Difficulty Controlling His Lust Towards Men (Especially Towards The Young Novice Who Had Just Joined The Monastery), The Young Novice Who Had Just Joined The Monastery And Who Was Still Confused About His Sexual Identity, and The Old Monk Who Had A Childlike Belief In Everything Offered By His Faith And Who Was A Bit Educationally Subnormal.

Charles Paris had got the short straw of Brother Benedict, The Monk Who Just Listened To All Of The Other Monks Who Maundered On In Long Speeches About Their Own Internal Conflicts. Most of Charles's lines were 'Really?' and 'Did you?' It was one of those parts, like Horatio in *Hamlet*, where the actor playing it knows that everyone else onstage is having more fun than he is.

And where did The Girl fit in? She was a rape victim, who had escaped the carnage of the wars that swirled around outside, to seek sanctuary in the monastery. And, of course, she was a plot device, the stranger whose arrival changed everything. Her presence disrupted the serenity of an all-male society, to reveal the seething suppressed passions beneath.

On the title pages, below the cast list, was printed: 'The action takes place in any time – it could be now', which Charles thought was rather coy. He was wary of plays set in an unspecified time zone. Playwrights who wrote them claimed that this gave their work 'universality', but Charles knew this wasn't the real reason. By giving his play a timeless setting, Seamus Milligan had avoided having to do any research into contemporary politics or the way in which a real monastery might be run.

Charles Paris's view, on finishing the script, was that *The Habit of Faith* was pretty deadly. In fact, a seriously crap play. If he had any pride – or indeed the income to sustain any pride – he should have got straight on to Maurice Skellern and said he didn't want to do it. But . . . anything with Justin Grover in it would put those bums on seats. And a guaranteed three-month run in the West End was a guaranteed three-month run in the West End. A bit of stability, both geographical and financial, could only help the progress of his current rapprochement with Frances. He'd do it.

Before the read-through for *The Habit of Faith* started, at a rehearsal room in White City, Charles had been intrigued as to how Justin Grover would play things. Knowing the star's propensity for meticulous planning, there was a reasonable chance that he would just mumble through the text, with a view to working privately on his part in the course of the rehearsal period.

But it became clear that his preparation had already been done. As soon as the read-through started, Justin's interpretation of Abbot Ambrose was firmly in place. Every intonation, every nuance was fully formed. At times, although they were all seated, he could not stop himself from doing some of the hand gestures on which he had worked so assiduously.

What was more, to the dismay of all the other cast members, he already knew every line. Throughout the read-through, he didn't open his script once.

This was partly showing off, partly gamesmanship, but more importantly a statement of power. Justin Grover's performance was already there and immutable. The rest of the cast would have to fit their performances around it.

And the director's vision of the play would also have to be adjusted to match that of its star.

The person taking on the directing role had been very carefully chosen – and Charles felt pretty sure that it had been Justin Grover who had done the choosing. Nita Glaze was very much up-and-coming. Having done lots of theatre while at Manchester University, she had set up her own company, Chip and Pin, soon after graduation. Five years of touring the country and maintaining a strongly controversial presence on social media had raised her profile to the point where she started being offered assistant director jobs at some of the major regional theatres. The unwillingness of most directors to share their artistic vision made these fairly thankless postings, but they all helped build up Nita's CV. Soon she progressed to directing her own shows at various well-known London pub theatres and other venues. She became a regular arts commentator on Radio 4's *Front Row*, and even once appeared on television's *Newsnight*. Critics hailed her as a rising star.

The Habit of Faith would be her first West End production.

Giving her the job was a bold choice by Justin Grover, but a canny one. Media coverage would praise the appointment of someone young, vibrant and female, instead of the usual middle-aged, male 'safe pair of hands'.

And, to tick another of the right boxes, Nita Glaze was black.

In spite of her impressive credits, however, she was very inexperienced at the level of directing a major West End show. And of dealing with a star. Her previous work had demonstrated a shrewd eye for spotting talent and developing nascent careers, but that was a very different matter from dealing with someone as established as Justin Grover. He had such a clear idea of how he wanted things done, that it would take an exceptionally dominant personality to make him change a single intonation. Though strong-willed and confident, Nita Glaze did not have that kind of strength.

Her room for manoeuvre had also been circumscribed by the fact that the producers – or more likely Justin Grover himself – had appointed a designer with whom he had worked many times before. So, although there had been some illusion of consultation with Nita in the run-up to the start of rehearsal, she found herself in nominal charge of a production in which the set and the central performance had already been decided before she came on board.

Charles Paris knew there were two options for someone in that situation. Nita Glaze could either try to impose her own vision on the play, make every rehearsal an argument which she was ultimately bound to lose; or she could zip her lip, put on the show that Justin Grover wanted to be put on, and later reap the benefit of having had her credit on a major West End production. Charles knew what he'd do in the circumstances. But then he'd always done anything to avoid confrontation. He wondered whether Nita Glaze would have the good sense to do the same.

Anyway, there were no open conflicts at the read-through. Everyone was charming to everyone else. The official proceedings started with a welcome from the producer, saying what an exciting adventure they were all embarking on. Then Justin Grover also said a few words, confirming what an exciting adventure they were all embarking on.

In the general milling around which had preceded the start of the read-through, the star had greeted Charles warmly, 'Hello. I'm Justin Grover.'

He recognized this trick of old. It was a form of inverted egocentricity, whereby a famous person humbly maintains the illusion that no one knows who he is.

'I know that, Justin. You may remember that we worked together in Bridport. I was Rosencrantz and you were Guildenstern – or possibly the other way round.'

'Yes, of course I remember, Charles. But I thought you might have forgotten.'

This was taking mealy-mouthed humility a bit too far for Charles's taste, but he didn't make any comment. Just said a conventional, 'Anyway, I'm delighted to be working with you again.'

Justin Grover shrugged magnanimously. 'If an actor can't help out an old chum, what has the world of theatre come to, eh?'

Charles winced inwardly. He had never liked being patronized. There was no false humility from the star now. Justin Grover was saying unequivocally, 'I got you this job, and it therefore behoves you to be eternally grateful to me.'

Charles had known, from the various emails that had been sent around to the cast in the weeks running up to the read-through, that he'd be working with at least one other actor he knew. The part of Brother Philip, The Monk Who Had Difficulty Controlling His Lust Towards Men (Especially Towards The Young Novice Who Had Just Joined The Monastery) was being played by Tod Singer.

Charles had had an initial reaction of surprise when he saw this casting, because Tod wasn't gay. But then he had to remind himself that the encroaching political correctness, which would not allow actors to play parts of different ethnicity from their own, had not yet reached sexual orientation. And, when he came to think about it, he realized it never would. Insisting that gay parts could only be played by gay actors might gain some support, but the suggestion that gay actors should not be allowed to represent heterosexuals onstage would really flutter the dovecots. The classical canon contained far too many juicy roles of rampant womanizers. If gay actors were forbidden from playing parts like Othello – and indeed Hamlet . . . well, there'd be rioting on Shaftesbury Avenue.

Charles and Tod Singer had last worked together on *The School for Scandal* in Glasgow. Though it had not been the greatest production in the history of theatre ('Charles Paris's Benjamin Backbite lacked backbone.' *Glasgow Herald*), the two actors had become close friends, or at least assiduous drinking companions. Indeed, Charles had no recollection of drawing a sober breath from the first day of rehearsal to the last night party.

And, though of course, as part of the re-wooing of Frances, he was going to cut out the booze, it was still reassuring to know that Tod Singer would be in the company.

During the read-through, Charles did what everyone else was doing, looked covertly round the table to assess the people with whom he would be spending the next four months of his life. They had each identified themselves in the round-the-table ice-breaking exercise with which Nita had begun the morning, but he hadn't retained many of the names.

The playwright, Seamus Milligan, was a dour-looking individual, whose expression suggested he was suffering from some terrible mental burden. Catholic guilt, Charles reckoned. Only a Catholic, or a lapsed Catholic (which, in terms of guilt-bearing, was pretty much the same thing) could have created a play like *The Habit of Faith*. To write all that maundering-on about belief and the obstacles to belief, you had to think that religion mattered. Something which Charles Paris, from his early teenage years, had signally failed to do.

Back then, though, he had, for maybe eighteen months, had a deep, almost passionate faith. In retrospect, he reckoned it was a reaction against his parents' laid-back scepticism. Had his parents been believers, he would probably have found atheism earlier. But for those months of devotion, he did read a chapter of the Bible every night before sleep. He had even written into his copy a quote he'd got from somewhere:

This book will keep me from sin.
Sin will keep me from this book.

Then, one morning, aged about fourteen, Charles Paris had woken up with the conviction that he didn't believe any of it. And since then, he had not been troubled by religious doubt – or indeed religious thought of any kind.

All he had gained from the experience was a devoted admiration for the cadences of the Authorized Version. And he was sure that reading that beautiful language so early had helped him in his career as an actor. It developed his natural understanding of emphasis and rhythm.

His loss of faith had not turned him anti-religion. He had a great respect – even envy – for people with a faith. It just didn't work for him. Every time he had to go into a church – which was now more for funerals than weddings or christenings – he still hoped that something would happen. A divine revelation. A Damascene conversion. The heavens opening and God reaching down to claim Charles Paris for His own. But, sadly, nothing. He always felt on his exit from the church exactly as he had felt on his entrance.

Read-throughs are always an opportunity to assess the comparative talent of other company members. However much actors talk about being 'part of an ensemble', they are all ferociously competitive. Beneath the smarmy compliments they pay to each other, there is very often the burning conviction that 'I could play that part a lot better than he/she is doing.'

And Charles Paris had no doubt that he could play the part of The Monk Who Had Difficulty Controlling His Lust Towards Women much better than the actor who had been cast in the role. In fact, he reckoned a plank of wood or a bowl of porridge could play the part better.

He had retained, from the round-the-table introductions, the name of this talent-free individual. Grant Yeoell. He could recognize that, although useless as an actor, the young man was extraordinarily handsome. And nobody could maintain a physique like that without frequent visits to the gym.

What Charles didn't know, and what most of the rest of the world who watched *Vandals and Visigoths* could have told him, was that Grant Yeoell was involved in the franchise, playing the part of Wulf, the illegitimate son of Sigismund the Strong. Like many film actors, he had been cast originally for his looks. And, like many film actors, the fact that he couldn't act for toffee didn't matter. In the movies, the takes of scenes are so short, and the skills of editors so advanced, that, even without resorting to CGI, the aforementioned plank of wood or bowl of porridge could be made to give a convincing performance. And that was the case with Grant Yeoell.

So far as the producers of *The Habit of Faith* were concerned, whether he could hack it on stage or not was completely irrelevant. The sight on a poster of Grant Yeoell's name, in conjunction with that of Justin Grover, would put even more bums on seats. And who cared if those bums belonged to hormonally rampant underage girls? Or people dressed as Vandals, Visigoths or Skelegators? Producers, generally speaking, don't care about the quality of the people sitting on their seats, just the quantity.

Inevitably, in his checking-out observation of the read-through table, Charles Paris clocked The Girl. The name of the person playing the part (as he thought of her, thus avoiding the actor/actress dilemma) had stayed with him from the introductions. Liddy Max. From the way she read, she was clearly a very talented actress. And she had the kind of looks which could have propelled her to the top in the theatre, even if she didn't have the talent. Trim figure, fine blonde hair cut short, and the kind of large blue eyes in which many men would in time lose themselves.

Charles felt a knee-jerk – but pointless – rush of disappointment when he noticed she was wearing a wedding ring.

Why did he always react like that? It wearied him. Why could the sight of a pretty woman always set the same inevitable thoughts in train? Why could he not look at any woman without assessing her on some scale of fanciability? When he was in a good mood, such a reaction reassured him that he was still alive. When he was in a bad mood, it made him feel like a dirty old man.

Idly, he wondered how she had come to be playing The Girl in *The Habit of Faith*. Charles now knew that his own presence in the company was due to the magnanimity of Justin Grover. He wondered what kind of favour the star had been repaying when Liddy Max had been cast. It could be sexual, perhaps, but he wouldn't have expected Justin to be quite so obvious.

Charles had never really known about Justin Grover's sex life. He wasn't gay. Indeed, he was frequently photographed with some new starlet on his arm. His affairs kept the gossip columns well fed. But none lasted. Three months seemed to be their maximum duration. That had been the case when Charles had first known the actor in Bridport, and the same pattern seemed to have been repeated many times since. Justin had always been more interested in having some photogenic younger woman on his arm than in having relationships.

Charles's cynical view was that the star was too obsessed with himself to have any love to spare for anyone else. His sex life, like his acting, was a bloodless technical exercise, whose sole aim was to create an effect.

Charles found himself wondering whether Justin put his characteristic meticulous preparation and attention to detail into his bedroom activities. The image was such an unappealing one that he dismissed it from his mind.

And concluded that sex was unlikely to have played a part in the casting of Liddy Max. There must have been some other reason why Justin Grover had approved her. Charles wondered what it might be.

He took another surreptitious look across the table at The Girl. She was not yet out of her twenties. Far too young for him, he concluded wistfully.

There was another girl, who was introduced as 'ASM and under-studying Liddy'. Her name was Imogen Whittaker. A stunning natural redhead, she carried herself with striking ease and confidence. But she was even younger than The Girl.

The stage manager, Kell Drummond, though, was a much more interesting prospect. Forties, short black hair, strong but ample body, and that air of pragmatic competence which Charles never failed to find alluring. In his experience, stage managers had always been encouragingly pragmatic about sex, too.

Not, of course, that that had any relevance for him in his current situation. No, no, he told himself.

On the other hand, if he *had* still been interested in women other than his wife, he might have envisaged intriguing possibilities with Kell Drummond.

Long habit had ensured that, the morning of the read-through, Charles Paris had, on his journey from the tube station to the rehearsal room, noted the location of the nearest pub. And it seemed logical to adjourn there once *The Habit of Faith* had been read.

Rehearsal proper was scheduled to begin the following morning. The afternoon would be devoted to some necessary technical activities. With the read-through table removed, the stage management would lay down tape on the floor to mark out the dimensions of the single set. Some of the actors were required to stay and be measured up for their costumes, though Charles had assumed that monks' habits were one-size-fits-all. Later, there would be a production meeting for Nita Glaze and all the stage crew. Significantly, Charles noticed, Justin Grover said he too would be attending that. Slight pique tugged at the mouth of the director when she heard his announcement. Was there going to be no area of the production where she wasn't under surveillance?

Charles wasn't called for anything in the afternoon, so, after the rehearsal broke up, it seemed logical to invite Tod Singer to join him in the pub. 'Recapture the spirit of Glasgow, eh?'

Time had not been kind to his fellow actor. Tod would certainly no longer have fitted into the costume he wore as Snake in *The School for Scandal*. Mind you, Charles would no longer have fitted into his Sir Benjamin Backbite costume either. But Tod's face had aged too; it wore the corrugated complexion of a heavy smoker. And there was something haunted about his eyes. Which certainly

suited the part of Brother Philip, The Monk Who Had Difficulty
Controlling His Lust Towards Men (Especially Towards The Young
Novice Who Had Just Joined The Monastery).

Tod's reaction to the pub invitation was not as instant as it would
once have been. He seemed to be enduring some moral conflict
before he replied, 'Very well, OK.'

Charles prided himself on his memory for the favourite tipples of
his drinking companions. He remembered from the many sessions in
Bridport that he and Tod would start with pints of bitter and whisky
chasers, before possibly sharing a bottle of red wine and more Scotch.
So, at the bar he pointed to the logo of one of the bitters and said,
'Two pints of that, please.'

'No,' said Tod Singer.

'What?'

'Just a fizzy water for me.'

'Oh?'

'I've given up the booze.'

'For how long?'

The reply came back instantly. 'Three years, seven months and
fourteen days.'

This didn't sound promising. 'So, if you're not drinking, why
did you agree to come to the pub with me?'

'To test myself,' said Tod Singer. 'To see if I can be strong in the
company of the people with whom I used to share my deadly habit.'

Oh, great, thought Charles Paris.

THREE

C harles was less than impressed at being used by Tod as some barometer of rectitude. Without comment, he ordered the fizzy water and a pint for himself. He also took vindictive pleasure in adding a double Bell's as a chaser.

'So, what's all this about?' he asked, once they had sat down with their drinks.

And his friend told him. At length. There is an old adage that 'anyone who breaks a habit generally frames the pieces', and it certainly applied to Tod Singer. The drinking, which had started as recreational – and indeed Charles had thought of it as recreational back in Glasgow days – had gradually got out of hand until the next drink had become the greatest imperative in Tod's life.

It had started to affect his career. From being a reliable jobbing actor, who was never going to be a big star but who never experienced more than the odd month out of work, Tod Singer quickly gained a reputation as someone who was 'not so good in the afternoon'. Offers of work dried up, and on the rare occasions when he was employed, increasingly he failed to deliver. The point of no return came when he was sacked for being drunk onstage and slurring his words as Feste in a production of *Twelfth Night* in Bristol.

Round the same time, Tod's marriage had broken up. His ex-wife, for reasons he could now fully understand, turned him out of the family home. He was reduced to sleeping on the sofas and floors of friends. He had no work, nor – given the speed with which news travels round the world of theatre – any prospect of any. Being drunk onstage – or, to be more accurate, allowing being drunk onstage to affect one's performance – was one of the final disqualifications for an actor. No director was going to cast someone with that kind of reputation.

After six months of this, drinking even more, being unable to face the day ahead without a few morning slugs of vodka, Tod decided that he had a choice. Either he could spiral on down to his death, an unsanitary one on the streets or possibly suicide (it would be hard to tell them apart), or he could take on the challenge of cutting out alcohol altogether. He had gone for the second option.

So then he began to chronicle his way out of the morass into which he had descended. This second stage of the narrative also went on for some time. Charles had needed to break into it to make a return trip to the bar for a second pint and a second large Bell's chaser – Tod was hardly halfway down his fizzy water.

A sense of reassurance had settled on Charles. Yes, he knew he drank too much, but he'd never been in the straits that Tod Singer was describing. More than a few times he'd gone on stage in a condition that would have disqualified him from driving a car, but only rarely had his performance been compromised. There was some power, rather like the healing powers of 'Doctor Theatre', which sobered an actor up the minute he got under the lights.

Or so Charles Paris believed. So, though the recital he was listening to was undoubtedly boring, he found it comforting as well.

It turned out that the salvation of Tod Singer had been Alcoholics Anonymous. After many failed attempts to control his drinking by his own willpower, he had been taken to a meeting with a friend who shared the same problem. The path to abstinence had not been an easy one. There had during the early stages been many backslidings, but eventually the programme had worked. He was still an alcoholic, he would always be an alcoholic, but he had found the resources to resist the temptations of the booze. As he insisted on repeating, Tod Singer had now not had a drink for three years, seven months and fourteen days. And tomorrow he would not have had a drink for three years, seven months and fifteen days.

Charles was surprised how strong his reaction was to this narrative of redemption. It didn't make him feel moved to empathy or congratulations. It made him feel rather angry.

It also made him drink quicker. He was near the end of his second pint and the second chaser was long emptied. Just when Charles was wondering whether his companion might offer to buy him a drink, Tod looked at his watch.

'Still, good you're back in work now,' said Charles. '*The Habit of Faith.*'

'Yes.'

'Is it the first job you've done since—?'

'Good Lord, no. AA hasn't just been the salvation of my health.

I've also made some very good contacts there. You'd be surprised how many directors and producers there are at the meetings.'

When he thought about it, Charles wasn't surprised at all.

'Which also means,' Tod went on, 'word gets around the business that I'm now dry. Other directors start believing it's safe to cast me again. I haven't had a drink now for three years, seven months and fourteen days.'

Charles was getting a bit sick of this pious mantra. Presumably, like a rubber date stamp, Tod Singer's mind had to be recalibrated every morning to add another day. Time to change the subject. 'Have you worked with Justin Grover before?'

'Way back. Bridport, it was.'

'Oh, I worked with him there. Gave my Rosencrantz to his Guildenstern – or possibly the other way round.'

'Justin got a lot of work down there. Great mates with the director . . . can't remember his name.'

Charles couldn't either. Oh dear, was this a sign of early onset Alzheimer's kicking in? He seemed to remember reading somewhere that forgetting people's names was one of the first symptoms. Mind you, he had forgotten where he'd read it.

'So, did you audition for the part of Brother Philip?' he asked.

'No. funny thing . . . I just had a call from my agent out of the blue. I was offered the part. Needless to say, I took it. Four months on West End money . . .'

He didn't need to finish the sentence. For some reason, Charles didn't volunteer the fact that his experience had been identical. Was it just insecurity on Justin Grover's part – this need to surround himself with people he'd worked with before? Though quite a long time before . . .

Anyway, the topic was not pursued, as Tod Singer stood up. 'I must be on my way.' Then he said, with pride, 'I've been here for more than half an hour. That's the longest I've managed to stay in a pub since I started with AA.'

Bully for you, thought Charles. What am I supposed to do – give you a bloody medal? He too got up and made his way to the bar.

'See you in the morning,' said Tod.

'Sure.'

'Oh, and, Charles . . .'

'Yes?'

'If you ever seriously want to deal with your problem . . .'

'My problem?'

'. . . I'd be happy to take you along to a meeting.'

'An AA meeting?'

'Yes, of course.'

Without any response to his departing friend, Charles attracted the barman's attention. He didn't bother with the pint this time, just the large Bell's. As soon as he'd received the glass, before the ice had had a chance to chill its contents, he downed it in one and ordered another of the same. That he took back to his seat.

He pulled *The Times* out of his pocket. It was already folded back to the crossword. On his tube journey from Queensway to White City that morning, he'd been too nervous about the read-through to fill in more than a couple of clues. Now, in the pub, his concentration was also shot to pieces. It wasn't the booze, he was certain of that. It was anger engendered by his recent conversation with Tod.

The patronizing tone was what had infuriated him. All right, Tod Singer had had a serious drink problem and he was dealing with it. Well done. But for him to treat Charles Paris as though he were in the same category of need was presumptuous and insulting. To offer to take him along to an Alcoholics Anonymous meeting . . . Charles seethed.

His angry thoughts were interrupted by the arrival in the pub of a familiar figure. Seamus Milligan had slipped furtively through the door, and looked around, hoping not to encounter anyone he knew. The sight of Charles was a disappointment to him.

In quieter moods, Charles would have let the writer sit and drink on his own, but the booze had made him uncharacteristically expansive. 'Seamus, hi!' he called across the room. 'Let me get you a drink!'

Seamus came unwillingly towards him.

'What will you have?'

'Pint of Guinness, please.'

Charles went to the bar to get the order. Since a double Bell's went down so much quicker than a pint, he ordered another one.

He sat down opposite the writer. 'Great play,' he lied. 'Read really well, didn't you think?'

'Bits of it sounded all right,' Seamus Milligan conceded grudgingly.

'Is it something you've been working on for a long time?'

'A few years.'

'And you've never actually had any experience of being a monk?'

'No.'

Which explained, as Charles had suspected, why the monastic background was so imprecisely sketched in. 'But you clearly know all about the Catholic stuff?'

'Yes.'

'Brought up a Catholic, were you?'

'Yes.'

There was a silence. The writer was not about to volunteer anything. Charles persisted. 'And now . . .?'

'Lost my faith.'

'But don't they always say: "Once a Catholic" . . .?'

'Do they?'

This was not the most fruitful conversation of Charles's lifetime. 'Still, brilliant to get your play on in the West End, isn't it?'

'Oh, yes.'

'Have you worked with Justin before?'

'Way back. He was in a play I wrote that was done in Bridport.' Bridport again. 'I wrote a few for down there. Anyway, the one I did with Justin . . . Hopes of it going to the West End, but nothing happened . . .'

Seamus spoke as if nothing happening to his plays was a common occurrence.

'I worked at Bridport. The Imperial. What was the name of the guy who ran it?'

'Damian Grantchester was artistic director when I was there.'

'Yes, of course, that was his name.'

'He directed *The Damascene Moment.*'

'That was your play?' From the title – and from listening to *The Habit of Faith* that morning – Charles didn't imagine it had been a barrel of laughs.

'Yes.'

'And did Justin play the lead?'

'No, no. He was playing a very minor role.'

'Oh?'

'It was before he got starry.'

'Ah. It was at Bridport that I first worked with him.'

This prompted no response, so Charles didn't have to repeat his

Rosencrantz and Guildenstern routine. With an air of finality, Seamus Milligan drained his glass of Guinness and put it down on the table. He rose, suddenly very anxious to leave.

'Sorry, got to go. I'll return the compliment another time.'

'Fine.' Charles mused, 'Funny, you know, the Bridport connection with Justin. Me and Tod Singer, you . . . Makes me wonder if—'

'Nothing happened in Bridport!'

The ferocity with which the words were said, and the speed with which Seamus Milligan went out of the pub, left Charles in a state of puzzlement. Also with the feeling that he'd like another drink.

Rehearsals for *The Habit of Faith* ran pretty smoothly. Nita Glaze, as Charles had suspected she would, did not try to impose herself too much on the production. She was skilled in the mechanics of directing, she blocked the play sensibly and was liked by the cast. She seemed, even more importantly, to be liked by the backstage crew. A director who irritated the stage manager or wardrobe or the lighting designer could find their life made very difficult. But Nita was tactful and engendered a good company spirit.

The notes she gave to the actors were practical and encouraging, though Charles was always aware of the way she was constantly checking Justin Grover's reaction to what she said. He suspected that the two of them had private sessions at the end of the day's rehearsal, where the star would brief his director about his overall plans for the production.

But Justin almost never argued with her publicly. He was a quiet, respectful presence in the rehearsal room, and meekly accepted the notes that he had instructed his director to give him.

There was only one occasion when the company in the rehearsal room witnessed dissension involving their star. Nita was blocking the very beginning of *The Habit of Faith*, a dramatic scenario which Charles found rather unsubtle, though he had no doubt that it would work effectively with an audience.

The tabs rose on the stage in total darkness. Bells rang, not a cheerful carillon of celebration, but ominously repeated single notes of different frequencies. As they did so, lights above slowly grew in intensity to reveal the full cast, in a line facing front. By some accident of casting – Charles couldn't believe it had been deliberate – all the male cast members were more or less the same height. They were dressed in their habits, faces hidden under their cowls.

One by one, in time to the intoning of the bells, the monks pulled off their hoods to reveal their faces. All revealed male, tonsured heads, until the last in the row. That was Liddy Max, and when she uncovered herself, abundant (courtesy of the wig department) blond hair would ripple down over her shoulders in a mini-*coup de théâtre*.

But as Nita was blocking this scene, and lining the cast up onstage in the order specified on their scripts, Justin Grover said, 'Oh, I thought we'd agreed a change here.'

'I don't think so,' said the puzzled director.

The star looked out towards the stage manager's desk, next to which sat Seamus Milligan, sullen and crumpled with his script on his knee, as he would throughout the rehearsal process. 'I thought we'd agreed this, Seamus,' said Justin. His tone was even, but it carried authority.

'No,' the writer responded truculently. 'We can't spoil the play's first authentic moment of drama.'

He sounded as if he was preparing himself for a stand-up row, but all he got from the star was a subdued 'Hm.' Nita Glaze continued her blocking of the opening line-up with Liddy Max as the final unmasking.

But, significantly, at the next day's rehearsal, very early on in proceedings, the director said, 'I've had a bit of a rethink on the opening of the show. It seems to me that making The Girl the final reveal is a bit obvious, not to say sexist. To me it'd make more sense if we change the order, so we have The Girl in the penultimate position, get our audience reaction to that, and reveal that the last unknown character is Abbot Ambrose. He, after all, is the puppet master, a bit like Prospero, really . . . you know, the one who controls the action. I think the dramatic integrity of the play would be strength-ened by having him as the final reveal. So, can we try that, please?'

Charles could see the suppressed anger in Seamus Milligan's body language as the new order was rehearsed, but the playwright made no vocal objection. Nor did any other member of the cast. Clearly, some overnight discussions had taken place. Nita and Seamus had been persuaded that *The Habit of Faith*'s 'dramatic integrity' would be incomparably improved by letting Justin Grover steal the end of the first scene.

And, Charles thought cynically, the star had probably already calculated that the first sight of him each performance would prompt a round of applause from fans of Sigismund the Strong.

But Nita Glaze had made the idea for the change sound completely as if it was her own. Maybe the girl had a future as an actor as well as a director.

Meanwhile, after that small ruffling of the surface, the harmonious process of rehearsal flowed smoothly on.

There was only one company member with whom Nita Glaze did not seem to bond, and that was Liddy Max. Whether this was a gender issue, Charles did not know. He had long since given up trying to understand what caused some women not to get along. There seemed to be so many complex layers of slight and counter-slight in their relationships, it was confusing for a mere male. Maybe there was just an instinctive antagonism between the two young women, both in their twenties. Or maybe Nita felt more confident being dictatorial to someone of her own sex and age than she did to the male cast members, most of whom were considerably older and more experienced than her.

Their disagreements never erupted into open conflict, there was just an identifiable tension between them in the early days of rehearsal. Nita seemed to give more notes to Liddy than to the other cast members, particularly about her first big scene, in which The Girl has a long speech describing the assault and rape which has led her to seek sanctuary in the monastery. Maybe, as a woman, Nita felt that she could identify with that experience and was there-fore more sensitive to false notes in Liddy's interpretation.

Though the tension between the two of them did not dissipate completely, as rehearsals continued there was less open verbal disagreement. Charles Paris thought it highly possible that Justin Grover had had a word with his director.

FOUR

'Are you going to have a glass of wine now, Daddy?' asked Juliet.

They were sitting down to Sunday lunch in his daughter and son-in-law's five-bedroomed architect-designed house in Pangbourne, into which they'd moved from their previous three-bedroomed architect-designed house in Pangbourne. They had, needless to say, made the move at the most economically advantageous time and, as Juliet's husband kept telling anyone who'd listen, they'd paid off the mortgage on the new property early.

There had never been a natural affinity between Miles Taylerson and his father-in-law. Charles still wished his daughter had opted for someone with a bit more charisma. But he could not fault Miles as a husband or father. Since he'd married Juliet when she was nineteen, he had supplied her every need, providing the economic security which allowed her not to work after the birth of their twin sons.

This again rankled with Charles. He liked the idea of having a daughter with a career, not necessarily as louche a one as acting, but something vaguely creative. Miles, however, was very old-fashioned about such matters. He wanted a wife who looked after the house, and who was ready to welcome him every evening when he returned from his arduous day's work. The fact that Juliet didn't need to work also demonstrated, to Miles, his own career success. And, as Charles had had cause to observe on many occasions, his daughter seemed very happy with the arrangement. Though how she filled the days, particularly now that the twins were off at private boarding school, he had no idea.

Charles felt a residual guilt about the situation. Had he been a more hands-on father, had he been more present during her childhood, had he not walked out on Frances while Juliet was still a toddler, perhaps their daughter might have had more bravery with which to face the world. Perhaps she wouldn't have embraced at such a young age the stolid security that her husband offered. Was it a reaction against the unpredictability of her own upbringing? Still, it was far too late for such speculations to be useful.

Miles Taylerson was in insurance. No other career could have placed him further from the interests of his father-in-law. He was apparently very good at insurance, though Charles had no idea what kind of skillset would be useful to make one good at insurance. Miles had been along dutifully with Juliet to one or two of Charles's performances, but he had no interest in the theatre. Or any of the arts, really.

He did read books, though, but they weren't what Charles thought of as books. No fiction. They were all 'How To' books. Whenever Miles was introduced to something new, he read a book – or several books – about it. When he took up photography, he immersed himself in floods of data about focal lengths and shutter speeds. Taking up fishing, a hobby which he still pursued, had been preceded by much reading about tickler lures and swimfeeders.

The passage of time had thickened Miles around the waist and receded his hairline. He looked what he was, a complacent middle-aged, middle-class success in the world of insurance.

Through intermittent encounters over the years, the chalk and cheese that were Charles and Miles had managed to achieve a kind of relationship. Subjects for conversation were restricted to fishing, the doings of the twins, and generalities about the awful mess that was contemporary politics.

There were two things about his son-in-law, though, that no amount of time could prevent from aggravating Charles.

First, Miles persisted in trying to sell his father-in-law insurance policies and pensions all the time.

Second – and much worse – he insisted on calling Charles 'Pop'.

'So, are you going to have a glass of wine now?' Juliet repeated, drawing her father out of his reverie.

'What? Oh, well, I suppose I . . .' Charles caught Frances's eye. 'No thanks, I'm driving.'

Juliet looked gobsmacked. She had been surprised at the sight of her father refusing a drink before lunch. For him not to have one with the meal was completely unprecedented. 'You're not ill, are you?' she asked.

'No, no, fine. Just cutting down a bit.'

He was rewarded by an approving look from Frances. What he'd said was true. Following the terrible bender he'd been on after *The Habit of Faith* read-through, he had been cutting down a bit. Not as much as his wife would have liked, but there was a kind of progress. In the third week of rehearsal, he'd gone three days without an alcoholic drink. A small achievement by some people's standards, perhaps, but for Charles Paris it had been mould-breaking.

'Well done, Pop.' He winced. 'Seeing the error of your ways, eh?'

The last thing he wanted was to be patronized by his bloody son-in-law, but Charles restrained himself from making any comment.

'Still, good news you've got this job in the West End,' Miles went on. 'Three months' secure income, I gather?'

'Four, with rehearsal.'

'Even better.' There was a silence as Miles started to carve the joint of beef that Juliet had just produced from the kitchen. The meat on its tray and the accompanying dishes of vegetables looked like photographs from a television chef's recipe book.

The carver continued, 'This would, of course, be an excellent opportunity, Pop, while you're earning good money, to put a little away each month, to make some kind of provision for your future.'

'I'm not sure that I—'

'Our company does have a range of products which suit people whose income sources are erratic . . . you know, freelance people. Because I assume that you still haven't made any pension provisions for—'

'You assume correctly,' cut in the dry response.

'Well, it's never too late to make a start. Obviously, it would have been better if you had been more provident earlier in your career, Pop, but—'

'Miles . . .'

Charles caught Frances's eye and saw that she was suppressing a giggle. That discouraged him from launching into the diatribe he'd been about to unleash. Also, there was something rather appealing about sharing private jokes with his wife. It had a nostalgic charm. Though fiercely loyal to Juliet, Frances did recognize that the person their daughter had married was a complete prat.

'Anyway,' said Juliet, sensitive enough to know that the situation needed easing, 'when does the show actually open, Daddy?'

'Week after next.'

'Oh, great. We must get to see it, mustn't we, Miles?'

'Sure, poppet.' Charles was reminded of another of his son-in-law's infuriating verbal tics.

He noticed that neither of them paused to confirm the date of the opening night. They had no interest in seeing *The Habit of Faith*. Though, given the current thawing of their relationship, he thought Frances was likely to put in an appearance.

Demonstrating her loyalty, she asked, 'And you actually get into the theatre for the first time tomorrow?'

'Yes. The good old Duke of Kent's.'

'I can't remember, have you worked there before?'

'Don't blame you for not remembering. Show I was in closed within a week.' It wasn't one of his happier experiences. ('Charles Paris kept looking out over the audience, rather like General Custer, hoping to see the cavalry appearing over the hill. Sadly, no one arrived to save the evening.' *The Guardian*.)

'It's Shaftesbury Avenue, though, isn't it?' asked Frances.

'Oh yes, one of the old theatres in urgent need of a makeover. Musty old seats, miles and miles of steep stairs backstage.'

'So, has the set gone in over the weekend?'

He shook his head. 'Too expensive. Producers aren't going to pay the crew weekend rates. No, they start building it on Tuesday. Then we have a week of techs and previews.'

'Why are you going in tomorrow, if the set's not up yet?'

Charles shrugged. 'Star's command, Frances. Justin wants us to work in the empty theatre, so that he can "acclimatize himself to the space".'

'Justin Who?' asked Juliet.

'Justin Grover.'

'Oh, wow! He's brilliant in the *Vandals and Visigoths* series!'

'Bloody great!' Miles agreed.

So, thought Charles glumly, the success of Sigismund the Strong has even penetrated the thick, unartistic skull of my son-in-law. That really was global fame.

Frances dozed as he drove back to London. She'd had a couple of glasses of wine at lunchtime, though, as Charles kept virtuously reminding himself, he'd had nothing. When they'd been together in the old days, she would have driven.

She'd recently acquired a newer car, a blue Skoda Fabia. He found it quite easy to drive. The London-bound Sunday evening traffic was heavy, and he looked into the cars alongside. A lot of couples, preparing for the start of the working week in the morning.

To them, he and Frances must look just like another ordinary couple, married for years, never straying from their closeness.

The image was not without its appeal. Driving back from Sunday lunch with daughter and son-in-law. What could be more domesticated than that?

He reminded himself fondly that the day had started well. He'd stayed over the night before in Frances's flat and, in the morning, before setting off for Pangbourne, they'd made love. Again, very domesticated. Almost like being married.

He resisted the strong urge to have a drink when they got back to Highgate. He found, as he had on the other rare occasions he'd tried it, that if he could get through the six-to-eight time of need, not drinking ceased to be a problem.

It was boring rather than anything else.

So, that Sunday night he sat with Frances, watching some period drama on television. Television without a drink was boring too.

The plan had been for him to go back to his place, but she didn't object to the idea of his staying over another night. His call at the Duke of Kent in the morning wasn't till ten. Plenty of time to go back to Hereford Road, shower and change his clothes.

When they were both in bed, he snuggled up against her back. But when he moved his hands round to her breasts, Frances gently removed them. 'I'm tired,' she said.

Yes, it was just like being married.

FIVE

'OK, company, let's just all close our eyes and breathe in the atmosphere.'

It might have been thought that, once they'd reached the Duke of Kent's Theatre on the Monday morning, the director would be in charge. But no, it was Justin Grover who was giving the instructions. The cast had got used to this pattern during the rehearsal period. In the early days Nita Glaze had tried to impose her will on the production, but after a few set-tos with her star, she had given up the unequal struggle. She had evidently decided to grit her teeth until the show opened, and then reap the benefit of a West End credit on her CV.

It should be said that the 'set-tos' between director and star had not involved any shouting or flouncing. Justin Grover was not one of those actors who shouted or flounced. He just argued, very reasonably, that everything should be done the way he wanted it done. And, since the production of *The Habit of Faith* would not have been happening without his box-office appeal, very few people argued with him.

But he was very tactful with his director. Although his performance had been set in stone since long before rehearsals had started, he did make a few well-judged concessions to Nita. Occasionally, she would say something like, 'I think we could make that pause longer there' or, 'If you say the line after you've made the move, it might be more effective', and he would be fulsomely grateful for the suggestion. 'Oh, very good note, Nita,' he would say. 'Thank goodness we've got a director with a sharp eye in this show. If I was left to my own devices, the whole thing'd be a total shambles.'

Of course, what he was saying was complete nonsense and, although Nita basically knew it was nonsense, she glowed at the commendation. Nor did she ever object when Justin ignored the note and went back to doing what he'd always intended to do.

And now he had the entire *The Habit of Faith* company standing on the stage of the Duke of Kent's Theatre, closing their eyes and breathing in the atmosphere.

Though he thought Justin had sounded rather precious, Charles was not as impervious to the effect of what they were doing as his customary cynical manner might suggest. Just being in any theatre for the first time did energize him. The older and emptier that theatre was, the stronger the sensation he felt. There was a kind of magic in the backstage smells of size and dust, the mustiness of old upholstered seats. He felt a connection to all the other actors who had trodden those particular boards, and empathized with the triumphs and disasters, the tragedies and love affairs that the ancient walls had witnessed.

'OK, that's fine. You can open your eyes now.'

The company did as their star instructed.

'Excellent,' said Justin. 'Well, I've now got a feeling of the place, which is always terribly important to me, as an actor. But now, over to you, Nita, for the other things you called us to do.'

The director looked confused. It wasn't she who'd ordered the ten o'clock call at the Duke of Kent that morning. Justin Grover had issued the instruction to Stage Manager Kell Drummond. And now he was making it look as though the idea had been Nita's.

But she was a bright girl and recovered quickly. 'Yes, there are a few scenes I'd like to walk through,' she improvised, 'just to check the sightlines.'

It was a good thought, and a logical use of the whole company's presence in the theatre. Though they couldn't really be sure what could be visible and not visible until the set was in place, checking out some of the big scenes might be a useful exercise. And it would give Nita Glaze some credibility as the person who set up the call.

The actors who weren't required onstage took the opportunity to explore the space that would be their home for the next three months. Charles Paris wandered with interest around the backstage area, still in thrall to the magic of the building. Though he had never acted in the Duke of Kent's, he had on occasion visited friends who were in shows there, and he remembered the vertiginous steepness of the stairs up to the dressing rooms.

He also recalled the recurrent awkwardness engendered by such post-performance visits. Even if he hadn't told an actor that he was going to see the show, he knew it was still *de rigueur* to 'go round' afterwards. There was always a danger that a mutual friend might have reported his presence in the audience to the actor in question, prompting the desolate wail, 'You mean Charles Paris was there and he *didn't come round!*'

Whether he'd liked the show or not, he had always found backstage encounters excruciating. Though normally adequately articulate, on such occasions he became tongue-tied. There was something about seeing fellow actors on a high from having just done a show, of which he had not been part, that robbed him of words. What was the right thing to say? He had never resorted to Alan Bennett's recommendation of just saying 'marvellous' as many times as possible, but he had occasionally been guilty of using the actor's last resort, tapping his friend on the chest and murmuring, 'What about *you* then?'

Charles had been given the number of his dressing room, and located it on the second floor, up two flights of the steep stairs. When he got there, he found the door locked. No problem. He hadn't the energy to go down to get his key from the stage doorman. He would have plenty of time to get to know the place – possibly to get sick of the place – over the next three months. He drifted back downstairs.

On the first landing, he stood aside to let Liddy Max pass. She had been more thoughtful than he, and her dressing room key was in her hand.

'All right?' asked Charles, in the meaningless way one does ask, 'All right?'

'Good,' said Liddy.

'Been let off the hook, haven't we?'

'What do you mean?'

'No rehearsal this afternoon. And then one last night of freedom. Before we get locked in here for the next three months.'

'Oh, right.'

'So, what are you going to do with this precious bonus of time?'

'Enjoy it.'

'Who's the lucky man?' As soon as he'd said it, Charles knew it was a stupid question. And probably sexist. One had to be so careful these days.

But Liddy didn't appear to be offended, just chuckled and said, 'Wouldn't you like to know?' She was silent for a moment, then her face darkened as she volunteered, 'I've been through a bad patch the last year. But I'm beginning to see the light at the end of the tunnel. Things are turning round for me. Getting the part of The Girl, and then . . . Yes, the next year is going to be a whole lot better.'

'And this evening will be part of that getting better?'

'Sure will,' she replied very positively. 'See you.'

Liddy turned towards her dressing room, key at the ready. Charles set off down the stairs.

And, as he did so, he realized that Liddy had not been wearing a wedding ring. Whether that was important or not, he did not know, but he remembered distinctly that she had been wearing one at the read-through.

Charles sometimes worried that he was obsessed by wedding rings on women's hands. He often found himself craning round to see if passengers on the tube were wearing them. Watching interviews on the television news, he got frustrated by the fact that people tended to be framed from the chest up, so that their hands were out of sight, and only when they made gestures could the give-away ring be seen.

He felt pretty sure that his interest was not pervy. Nor was it a knee-jerk masculine availability check. He thought it was part of the mindset of an actor. Like writers, they had to be observant, they had to work out what made people tick. And an essential part of that process was providing backstories for them. Looking at complete strangers on public transport and trying to guess the life experiences that had brought them to that particular moment in time . . . Everyone did it to some extent, in an idly speculative way, but when an actor or writer did it, then that was *work*. Or so Charles tried to persuade himself.

Mind you, it was getting more difficult. He looked back to a time when wedding rings gave out a single, simple message: the female wearer of this ring is married to a man, or is possibly a widow. But now, with as many grooms wearing rings as brides, and same-sex couples exchanging them with their husbands or wives . . . Charles Paris frequently found modern life confusing.

From the foot of the stairs, he drifted towards the Green Room, where he found quite a few cast members had congregated. They were waiting to hear from the director that they'd been released. (One advantage of Justin Grover's having them called to the theatre meant that there was no more rehearsal scheduled for the day. It would be their last free evening, Sundays excepted, for the next three months.)

Kell Drummond was there, answering general queries from the company, most about the allocation of dressing rooms. There was of course no question which one Justin Grover would get, and the relatively small cast of *The Habit of Faith* meant that no one would have to share. But there were still a few niggles from actors who wanted more generous accommodation. Kell rose above this, not allowing any changes and announcing that, if anyone wanted to leave stuff in their dressing rooms that day, they could do so by getting the key from the stage doorman, who went by the unlikely name of Gideon.

As he had been at the read-through – and a few times since – Charles was struck by what an attractive woman Kell was. Again, he was drawn to her earthy pragmatism, so unlike the winsomeness evident in many actresses (or did he now have to say 'female actors'?).

Kell was stopped in mid-sentence by the ping of an arriving text. She checked her phone. 'OK, we're all done here. Nita's finished onstage. Next call will be two o'clock tomorrow afternoon, assuming the set's in by then. Two o'clock tomorrow, unless you hear to the contrary.'

It was amazing the speed with which everyone collected up their belongings and vacated the Green Room. Charles found himself alone with Kell, who was checking through some notes on her script. He looked at his watch. Just after two o'clock.

'I was thinking of grabbing a bite to eat,' he said. 'You've got time to leave the theatre, have you?'

'Since it's probably the last time I'll escape the place till the small hours of Wednesday morning – if then – yes, be a good idea to get some food inside me.'

She gave him a smile broad enough to set him wondering whether she smiled at everyone equally broadly, or was he receiving the privilege of extra broadness? He smiled back. Of course, he was devoted to Frances – he'd just spent the night with her, for heaven's sake – but there was no denying Kell's attractiveness.

'There's quite a nice pub round the corner that I used to go to when I was working at the Globe . . . that is, of course, when it was the Globe . . . before it was renamed the Gielgud. Before your time.'

The last words were said with a chuckle, but then he realized they were probably true. He couldn't remember exactly when the Globe had been renamed, but the stage manager must have been a good fifteen years younger than him. If not twenty.

'OK,' she said. 'But I'd better warn you, with the schedule I've got over the next couple of weeks, I can't drink.'

'Could you cope with watching me drink?'

Another broad grin and a nod. 'Once the show's up and running, I'm available for heavy drinking sessions every night after curtain down.'

That sounded like a promise. Charles grinned back. 'Come on then.'

Before they had made it out of the Green Room, Tod Singer and Liddy Max entered. A little way behind them came Imogen Whittaker. 'Hi, anyone going out to eat something?' asked Tod.

'We were just on our way,' said Kell.

'May we join you?'

'Sure,' she replied, giving Tod a broad smile. Charles wasn't quite sure whether it was as broad as the one he'd been granted, and didn't enjoy making the comparison.

'That's great. I'm starving. I'll soon be eating my hair,' said Liddy. 'You coming, Immy?' Her understudy nodded.

'Well, there's a very nice pub round the—'

But Charles's words were drowned out by Tod saying, 'Great sandwich bar dead opposite the stage door.'

'Sounds good,' said Kell.

'Brilliant,' said Liddy.

Outside, Charles was surprised to see a gaggle of some half-dozen teenage girls, giggling and waiting for something. He gave Kell an interrogative look.

'Grant Yeoell's fans. Or do I mean groupies?'

'Blimey. How did they know he was going to be in the theatre today?'

'No secrets these days with social media around.' Then drily, she added, 'Really, don't you know, Charles? It's official. Grant Yeoell is "Sex on Legs".'

'Oh, he's a lot more than that,' said Liddy Max.

Charles was constantly amazed by the mechanics of what made men attractive to women. He could recognize that Grant was reasonably good-looking, but couldn't really see why his images were so omnipresent on teenage girls' bedroom walls and mobile phone screens. The fact that the real Grant Yeoell was bone-headed and dull didn't seem to enter the equation.

Being a purely physical babe-magnet was not a problem that Charles had ever had to deal with. Any success he had had with women had been achieved by a nimble tongue and a genuine interest in the personality of the woman involved. Fortunate to be articulate and occasionally amusing, he was never going to get anywhere on raw sex appeal. Which was apparently what Grant Yeoell had.

Charles still found it strange, and he knew that, in such gender-sensitive times, he was probably being sexist to find it strange. In his time, he had not been unaffected by the charms of pin-ups and had never thought to enquire about their intellectual abilities. Why shouldn't women feel the same about masculine images?

Maybe there was also an element of jealousy at work there, too. It had become clear during some weeks of rehearsing with Grant Yeoell that the young man took full advantage of his magnetism. He had no ongoing relationship, but enjoyed as many guilt-free one-night stands as he could fit into his busy schedule.

Yes, Charles Paris was jealous.

Charles took a sip of his San Pellegrino sparkling water. It wasn't really what he'd had in mind. Nor were the tall stools pressed against the ledge in the sandwich bar window. He wasn't convinced by his crayfish and avocado panino either.

He thought wistfully of stretching his limbs out in the greater space of the pub, empty after the lunchtime rush, tackling a pint and some nourishing delicacy like sausage and mash.

But a tiny part of him felt virtuous. He wasn't having a drink. Frances would be proud.

Kell wiped her full lips as she finished her ham and cheese toastie, and asked the same question Charles had put to Liddy. 'So how're you lot planning to spend your last night of freedom?'

'Nothing special,' replied Tod. 'An AA meeting and an early night, I think. To prepare me for the rigours ahead.' He had no embarrassment about his dedication to Alcoholics Anonymous. Indeed, he seemed to make a point of bringing it into the conversation as often as he could. 'And you, Kell?'

'It's not my night of freedom. It's my night of listening to a lot

of foul language when the stage crew start blaming the designer for
the fact that the set doesn't fit.'

'Of course.'

'But, as you said,' Charles interposed, 'you'll be compensating
with many heavy drinking sessions afterwards.'

He knew the line was rather crass. He didn't know why he'd said
it. Well, he did, actually. It was a reaction against Tod Singer's pious
abstinence. There was also something sexual there too. He had
picked up a vibe that Tod was interested in Kell, and Charles wanted,
as it were, to claim her allegiance to the cause of the drinkers.
Allegiance to him too, perhaps.

'You got anything planned, Immy?' asked Kell.

The redhead's freckled face was irradiated by a smile. 'Meet up
with a few friends. Then early night too.'

'You, Liddy?'

Charles was keen to hear more about her plans, after the intriguing
hint she'd dropped backstage.

But before she could answer, Liddy looked out of the window
and saw someone she recognized. A thin young man in a blue
pinstriped suit stood outside. He had a flop of hair across his forehead and an expression of petulance.

'Sorry, excuse me a moment,' she said and hurried out.

As soon as she joined him, the young man engaged in heated
discussion with her. He seemed angry about something, and was
waving his arms around.

'Has Liddy got a stalker?' asked Charles.

'That's no stalker,' said Kell drily. 'That's her husband. Derek.
He was asking for her at the stage door earlier.'

They watched as Liddy and Derek walked off out of sight. The
girl's body language was now as angry as her husband's.

Kell Drummond looked at her watch and downed the remains of
her coffee. 'Back to the House of Fun,' she said. 'See you lot at
two tomorrow, unless you hear to the contrary.'

'We'll be there,' said Tod, and Kell gave him a broad smile.

'Sure will,' said Charles, and Kell gave him a broad smile. He
couldn't quite be certain, but he reckoned the one she'd given Tod
was marginally broader. Or was he being paranoid?

'I must go too,' said Imogen, gathering up her bag and adding
mysteriously, 'lots of things to sort out before this evening.'

After the women's departure, there was a silence between the two men. The easy camaraderie of their Glasgow days didn't seem equal to surviving Tod's sobriety.

'So how are you going to spend this unexpected leisure time, Charles?'

'Ooh, I don't know. But it might involve going to a pub and having a drink. I don't suppose you . . .?'

The expression on Tod's face gave him his answer. As he knew it would. Charles recognized he was being childish, goading his former friend by bringing up the subject of alcohol. He should be showing respect for Tod's self-control, rather than teasing him about it.

'No, no, I didn't really think you would. Instead, you're going to fill the idle hour with an AA meeting?'

'Yes.'

'How often do you do that?'

'Most days.'

'How long do they last?'

'Varies. Hour, hour and a half.'

'Do you have to go far?'

'You're usually quite near a meeting.'

'What, even when you're on tour?'

'Oh yes, if a town's big enough to have a theatre, there'll be an AA branch. In the West End of London, there's quite a choice.'

'Ah,' said Charles. Then he remembered a good story he'd heard. ' "Friend of mine had a drink problem. So bad he joined Alcoholics Anonymous. He still drinks, but under another name!" '

Tod's face demonstrated clearly that he didn't find the joke as funny as Charles did. 'You should try coming to a meeting.'

'What, me? Alcoholics Anonymous?'

'Why not? You've obviously got a problem.'

'Oh, come on, Tod. All right, yes, I drink a bit more than I should. But I haven't got a *problem*.'

'No?'

'No!'

'If you say so.' Tod's tone sounded, to Charles, smugger than ever. 'Anyway,' he went on, 'I must be on my way. If you change your mind about coming to the meeting . . .' He gave the address. 'Six o'clock. Only an hour this one. So that actors who've got performances can get in before the "half". There'll be a lot of people from "the business" there. Lots of people like you, Charles.'

With a sardonic smile, Tod Singer left the café. Charles went straight to the nearest pub.

He was nearing the end of his second pint – he'd already downed the second chaser – and not getting very far on an intractable *Times* crossword, when his mobile rang.

This was unusual. Having a mobile phone was essential for a contemporary actor. Who could say what time of the day or night might come the call from one's agent saying that the National Theatre wanted one to give one's Lear? Also, when one was actually in work, information from the stage management about rehearsal calls tended to come in the form of text messages. But those were the only reasons why Charles possessed a mobile. He wasn't interested in the many other facilities it provided. He didn't want to listen to music on a phone, or to Google, and his fingers seemed too big and clumsy to deal with the tiny keyboard. On the rare occasions when he sent emails, he used the laptop back in Hereford Road.

He wasn't like the generation of younger actors who checked their phones (and drank Perrier) the moment each rehearsal break was announced.

The call was from Frances. 'Hi, Charles. I was wondering how your schedule was working out.'

'My schedule?'

'Rehearsals. Don't you remember, this morning you said you might be free this evening and, if so, you'd take me out for dinner.'

'Oh, yes. Yes.'

'So are you?'

'What?'

'Free this evening?'

'Yes. Sure.'

'Well, then . . .?'

Charles had to readjust his plans for the day. He had indeed forgotten the morning's exchange with Frances, and had been contemplating, with some relish, a day's drinking. He was already under way on that, but if he stopped now, he told himself, he'd be sober by the time he met Frances.

'Yes. Sure,' he said again.

There was a burst of laughter at a punch-line delivered by one of a group of men at the bar. 'Where are you, Charles?' Frances asked suspiciously.

'Oh, just in a place having a drink. There's a break in rehearsal.'
Why was he lying to his wife? Long habit?

'By "a place", I assume you mean "a pub"?'

'No, just a coffee shop.' Oh God, another lie.

'I see,' said Frances, and he was rather afraid she did. But she
moved on. 'So, tonight . . . what time? Eight'd suit me.'

'Fine.'

'Usual place in Hampstead.'

'That'd be good.'

'OK, I'll book it. As you said this morning, your last free evening
for three months.'

He had forgotten saying that too, but responded, 'True enough.'
He chuckled. 'And I suppose you're expecting me to go through
the whole evening without an alcoholic drink?'

'Yes,' said Frances. 'I'm glad you're getting the message, Charles.'

It was nearly four by the time he left the pub. He would have stayed
there longer, but the call from Frances had prohibited his normal
way of killing time. Four hours till he needed to be in Hampstead.
Not worth going back to Hereford Road. He supposed there might
be a movie about to start in one of the cinemas around Shaftesbury
Avenue, but he didn't feel up to the effort of finding a newspaper
and checking the listings. (It didn't occur to him that that kind of
information could be easily accessed on a mobile phone.)

Then he remembered that for the next three months, he had a
pied-à-terre in the West End. His dressing room in the Duke of
Kent's Theatre.

The stage doorman, Gideon, was massively fat. His body spread
down into his chair like a jelly just released from its mould. But he
had a smile of universal beneficence, as he looked up from his
laptop to greet the new arrival.

'Hi. My name's Charles Paris.'

'Of course. Got your name on the list for *The Habit*.'

'That's right.'

'So, we'll be seeing a lot of each other over the next three months.'

'We certainly will.'

Charles had to squeeze up against the wall, as a bulky man
carrying a reel of electrical cable pushed through.

'So many people here for the get-in,' Gideon commented. 'In
and out through the scene-dock and here. I'm meant to get them to

sign in and out every time, but sod that for a game of soldiers. Just let them come and go as they please.'

'You have to,' Charles empathized.

The stage doorman nodded. 'Yes. Of course, I knew Justin Grover way back, just when he was starting his career.'

'Where was that?' asked Charles, thinking it'd be really spooky if the answer was Bridport.

But no. Gideon replied, 'RADA.'

'Did you act too?'

'Only for a few years. Don't think I was very good. Didn't get the parts, anyway. And then I had health issues.'

So maybe his huge bulk was due to some medical condition. Charles said, 'I'm sorry.'

'Don't be. The amount of sheer terror I've seen on actors' faces when they're coming in to do a show – be enough to put anyone off. I think I'm on the right side of the fence. And I get all the showbiz gossip sitting here, you know.'

'I bet you do.'

'I think I was only ever really in it for the gossip.'

Charles chuckled. 'Anyway, could I have my key? Got a couple of hours to kill.'

'Sure.' Gideon reached round to a board with numbered hooks on it. 'Seven. Nice dressing room. View into the kitchens of a Chinese restaurant. Apparently, Edith Evans once had it for a long run.'

'I will be appropriately respectful of her memory.'

'You do that.'

'Do you know, apparently once in rehearsal, Edith Evans thought the director was giving too much attention to working on one of the other actor's speeches, so she demanded: "And what am I supposed to do in this long pause while he's talking?"'

Gideon roared with laughter. He was a glutton for theatrical anecdotage, and Charles knew that his own impersonation of the Great Dame's strangled diction was rather good. Most actors had a few such tricks up their sleeves, and it was amazing how durable they could be. Long after their deaths, Green Rooms could still be silenced by impressions of Coward, Gielgud and Richardson.

Eventually, the laughter subsided, and Charles felt he'd made a useful ally. Gideon handed the key across. 'Make sure you give it back to me when you leave.'

'Will do.'

'And mind the stairs!'

Up in dressing room Number Seven, Charles settled into the chair in front of the bare mirror, and tried to focus his mind on *The Times* crossword.

He woke up feeling shitty. The afternoon's drinks had given him a headache which normally he would have dispelled by having more of the same, but the prospect of his rendezvous with Frances ruled that out. He felt in his pockets for paracetamol, but hadn't got any.

The fact that he hadn't completed any more of *The Times* crossword clues did not improve his mood.

In fact, he felt really depressed. He was ruining his life. He seemed to be on kamikaze autopilot. Frances had offered him a lifeline, and he seemed to be doing everything possible to avoid taking hold of it.

He thought about his drinking and, in his diminished state, realized that it was out of control. Left to his own devices that afternoon, he would probably have stayed in the pub for a couple more hours, then shambled back to Hereford Road, picking up a bottle of Bell's on the way. And there wouldn't have been much left in it by the end of the evening.

Tod Singer was right. He *had* got a problem.

He looked at his watch. Twenty to six. He remembered the address. Only five minutes away from the Duke of Kent's Theatre.

Maybe it was time he took back control of his life. Maybe it was time he attended an Alcoholics Anonymous meeting.

He bought some peppermint chewing gum on the way.

He didn't like it. The meeting took place in a church, which made him feel even more as if he were participating in the ritual of a religion, whose observances were unfamiliar. He had felt the same on the few occasions when he'd had to attend funerals in Catholic churches. He didn't know the responses, he didn't know the hymns, he didn't know when to stand up and when to sit down. He felt alienated by the congregation's smug familiarity with the routine. He felt everyone was looking at him.

The visit had started all right. Tod Singer had spotted him the moment he slunk into the church, and the greeting was genuinely warm. For him, Charles's appearance was no doubt a vindication. Another lost soul was being guided on to the path of righteousness.

But Tod reassured the visitor that he didn't have to say anything. 'You'll be offered the opportunity to tell everyone that this is your first meeting, but if you don't want to do that, then fine. Participate as much or as little as you want to.'

Tod had also introduced the newcomer to a lot of other attendees. Charles was taken aback by how many of them he already knew. He shouldn't really have been surprised. An AA meeting in the middle of Soho was, as Tod had suggested, bound to attract a lot of people 'in the business'. There were one or two present starry enough to have their names in lights on Shaftesbury Avenue, but there was no obeisance to professional hierarchy. Before the proceedings proper started, there were a lot of man-hugs, and a general feeling of slightly camp camaraderie. Charles found it quite appealing.

But once the meeting began, his attitude swiftly changed. It wasn't just the venue that made it feel like a religious service. On the wall behind the person in charge hung a scroll of the famous Twelve Steps, looking for all the world exactly like a manifest of the Ten Commandments. Obviously, the contents of the two lists were different, but Charles was surprised to see how much 'God' came into the Alcoholics Anonymous version.

He was also put off by the responses that the rest of the congregation knew so well. He had heard anecdotally about every comment being prefaced by 'I'm (INSERT FIRST NAME HERE) and I'm an alcoholic', but hearing it actually being said he found a big turn-off. The possibility that he might be adding to the conversation by saying, 'I'm Charles and I'm an alcoholic', already remote, quickly vanished over the horizon.

He found the congratulations offered when people announced how long they'd been without a drink, and the confessions they made of how the drink had ruined their lives, equally excruciating. Who cared about their lost jobs, their arrests, their relationships broken down by booze? They were a bunch of losers. Unlike him. He'd never let alcohol get in the way of anything really important.

Above all, he disliked the imposed sense of community. Charles Paris had never been a joiner. Maybe that was part of the problem.

The meeting certainly did not make him any likelier to give up alcohol. It made him, like a resentful child, even more determined to kick against this new expression of authority. An hour before, in his dressing room, Charles Paris would definitely have owned up to being an alcoholic. In that church, though, surrounded by the genuine article, he found his mind forming the words, 'You may be one, but I'm bloody not!'

Perversely, all the piety and bonhomie made him desperate for a very large Bell's.

However Charles Paris was going to achieve what Frances wanted of him, it wouldn't be through Alcoholics Anonymous.

When the meeting finally came to an end and the man-hugs and camp camaraderie turned to farewells, Charles thanked Tod Singer very much for inviting him.

'You don't have to go right now, do you, Charles? Why don't you join us round the corner for a coffee?'

He knew it was childish, but he couldn't help replying, 'No, thanks, Tod. I'm going to get a real drink.'

He was surprised at how angry he felt. The experience of the meeting had released a great flood of bile within him. Was it guilt? Or a deep unwillingness to be identified with the other sinners? Or resentment at having drinking identified as a sin?

He went straight to the nearest convenience store and bought a vastly overpriced bottle of Bell's.

Then back to the Duke of Kent's. The man-mountain Gideon was not in his cubbyhole, so Charles entered and took his key.

Then he went up to his dressing room and started drinking. Hard, destructive drinking.

He didn't know where he was when he woke up. His brain seemed to have shattered into hard, dry shards of flint that were grinding against each other. He reached for the bottle to ease the pain, and found it two-thirds empty. He took a long, restorative swig.

He had a feeling that things had happened during the evening. He'd met people, he'd talked to people. But his memory could not recall their names, their faces, or what they had talked about. He didn't know what was real and what was not real.

Charles looked at his watch. A quarter to eleven. And then he remembered Frances.

Clutching the bottle, in sheer panic he rushed down the vertiginous staircases.

At the bottom, at stage level, there was what looked like a pile of costumes. Closer inspection revealed it to be one of the monk's habits.

Inside it was Liddy Max. Blood from an unseen wound had reddened her blonde hair and pooled around her head.

She was dead.

That was real.

SIX

The stage door was again unmanned. Charles hung his key back on its hook and hurried out of the theatre.

He was in no condition to deal with Frances. He was in no condition to deal with anything. He hailed a cab and gave the driver the Hereford Road address.

Once there, he had to sleep. So he finished the bottle of Bell's.

The only good thing that happened on the Tuesday happened early. He received a text from Kell to say that there would be no rehearsal call that day.

Which was just as well because he was in no condition to deliver any kind of performance. To deliver anything, in fact.

He also found a series of increasingly anxious messages and texts from Frances. She had left them the previous evening. He must have been aware of the blips from his phone as they arrived, but known he was in no state to get back to her. He couldn't really remember.

In fact, he couldn't remember much of what had happened between his visit to Alcoholics Anonymous and his discovery of Liddy Max's body. The Bell's had blanked it out. From the self-righteous attitude with which he had separated himself from the other attendees at the meeting, his mood had spiralled down into despair and self-loathing. My name is Charles and I *am* an alcoholic.

He would have to ring Frances. She had sounded really worried about him. But as he had the thought, with it came a realization of the full awfulness of his behaviour. They had had a date at the Italian place in Hampstead. He had stood her up. He had left her sitting at a table on her own to suffer the pitying expressions of the waiters and other diners. In one evening of stupidity, he had undone all of the groundwork he had put into their rapprochement. There was no way now that Frances would reiterate her invitation to cohabitation.

He must ring her. But, as his trembling fingers reached towards the keypad, he was interrupted by the buzzing of his entry phone.

He lifted himself up to the vertical, realizing for the first time that he was still dressed as he had been the day before. He had no recollection of his taxi journey or of paying the driver, but he must have done it somehow. When he got back to the flat, presumably he'd just slumped on to the bed and passed out.

Standing up had not been a good idea. The room swam around him. The dried-up components of his brain shifted themselves into new contours of pain. He felt he was about to throw up. He wondered whether the contents of his mouth would smell as noxious to someone else as they did to him, and rather feared they would.

He picked up the entry phone. 'Hello?'

'Charles Paris?'

'Yes.'

'Police.'

There were two of them. Both male, neither in uniform. One tall, one short. They introduced themselves at the front door, but Charles didn't retain their names. He invited them in. Having moved books, papers and clothes off the only two chairs, he asked them to sit down. He perched on the edge of the bed. He had never felt less like being interrogated.

They told him they were investigating an 'incident' at the Duke of Kent's Theatre the night before. Charles had sufficient wits about him not to say something like, 'Oh, you mean what happened to Liddy Max?' No need to give them any more information than he had to. See how much they knew first.

'We gather,' said the short one, 'that rehearsal in the theatre finished around two yesterday afternoon.'

'That'd be about right, yes.' Charles had the feeling that he was on the verge of throwing up over both of them. That, he recognized, would not have helped his cause.

'But you went back into the theatre later.' He looked at them, trying to work out how much they knew, as the short one continued, 'The guy on the back door told us.'

'The *stage* door.'

'What?'

'Nothing.'

'His name's Gideon.'

'Yes, I know who you mean.'

'According to him,' said the tall one, consulting a notebook, 'you came back into the theatre round three.'

'Yes.'

'Why did you do that?'

'I had some time to kill.'

'"Time to kill",' echoed the short one, as though Charles had expressed the intention to murder someone. 'Why?'

'I was due to meet my wife in Hampstead at eight o'clock. It wasn't worth coming back here and then going out again.'

'No, I suppose it wasn't,' the short one conceded.

The tall one looked back at his notebook. 'And you left the theatre again at about a quarter to six.'

'Yes.'

'Leaving yourself plenty of time to get to Hampstead by eight o'clock.' The short one made it sound like an accusation.

'I didn't go straight to Hampstead.'

'No? Where did you go?'

There was no point in lying. There had been enough witnesses in the church to testify as to where he was at six o'clock. 'I went to a meeting of Alcoholics Anonymous.'

'Oh?' The taller policeman looked at the empty bottle of Bell's on the mantelpiece, and sniffed the air pointedly. 'Well, it doesn't seem to have done much good, does it?'

The short one, who seemed to be the senior of the pair, gave his partner a look of reproof. Clearly, accusing people you're interrogating of drinking too much did not conform with police guidelines.

'So, after the meeting, you went to Hampstead?' asked the short one, getting the questioning back on track.

'No.'

'Oh?'

'I didn't go to Hampstead.'

'Did your wife ring you to cancel the arrangement?'

'No. I just didn't go to Hampstead.'

'Oh,' said the tall one.

'So, what did you do?' asked the short one.

'I stayed in the West End, drinking.'

'And where did you do your drinking? In pubs? Clubs? Or did you go back to the Duke of Kent's Theatre?'

Faced with the direct question, Charles knew he had a choice. Gideon hadn't been on the door, either when he'd arrived at the theatre the second time, or when he'd left it. Not being involved in the investigation into Liddy Max's death seemed a much more attractive proposition than being involved in it. Charles had unpleasant experience of being questioned by the police. And his recollections of the evening were so hazy that he'd make a very unreliable witness.

'Just drank in various pubs,' he lied. 'Then came back here.'

The minute the words had come out, he knew he'd made a seriously wrong decision.

But neither of the policemen questioned his assertion. Instead, the tall one said, 'There was a break-in at the theatre last night.'

Again, the short one clearly disapproved of his colleague volunteering information.

'A break-in?' Charles echoed.

'The man on the back door was attacked.'

'Gideon?'

'That's his name, yes.'

'Is he seriously hurt?'

'Bruise on his forehead. He'll live.'

The short one chipped in, 'You didn't see the attack, Mr Paris?'

Having started out on the lie, he couldn't now go back on it. 'No. As I say, I wasn't at the theatre last night.'

'No.' There was a long silence. Charles was afraid his lie was about to be challenged, but instead, the short one asked suddenly, 'How well did you know Liddy Max?'

'Met her for the first time at the read-through for *The Habit.* That's the play we're doing. *The Habit of Faith.*'

'That's all?'

'What do you mean?'

'Have you seen much of her since?'

'Rehearsed with her a bit. Not much, because we don't have many scenes together.'

'But no contact outside work?'

Charles shook his head, not the best idea he'd ever had. As the contents of his cranium resettled themselves, he felt he ought to ask, 'Why? Has something happened to her?'

The policemen exchanged looks, and the tall one closed his notebook. The short one said, 'I don't think we need trouble you any more this morning, Mr Paris, but it's possible – even likely – that we'll need to talk to you again at some point.'

'Fine.'

'Here's a card with our contact details. Don't hesitate to call us if you think of anything relevant.'

'Relevant to what? You haven't told me what it is you're investigating. Can't you tell me what this is all about?'

'I think at this stage,' said the tall one, 'the less anyone knows about the detail, the better. Actors are, I've been led to believe, a gossipy lot.'

That earned another look of reproof from his superior. What had been said might be true, but this wasn't the moment to say it. The two turned to leave the cramped studio flat. Then the short one looked back. 'Oh, one thing, Mr Paris . . .'

'Yes?'

'Do let us know if you have any plans to leave the country.'

'I'm hardly likely to do that. I'm just about to start a three-month run in the West End.'

'True. But, if your plans change, let us know.'

He managed to see the two policemen out at the front door and then rushed up to his bathroom to throw up. But nothing came. Just dry retching that shook his body like an old bedframe.

He thought teeth-cleaning might improve the taste in his mouth, but his hand was shaking so much that he ended up with white paste all over his lips and chin. He wiped it off with a towel.

And next he knew he had to ring Frances.

But, before he could put that plan into action, his mobile bleeped to tell him a text had arrived.

'*If asked by police don't tell them if you came into the theatre yesterday evening. Please. Gideon.*'

His first question, in his fuddled state, was how the stage doorman had got his mobile number. But that was quickly rationalized. Kell Drummond would have given him contact sheets for all the company.

The text was still puzzling. Presumably Gideon didn't know that Charles had already spoken to the police. For reasons of his own, the stage doorman was warning him off disclosure of his movements the night before. In fact, requesting him to give the police exactly the mendacious account that he had given them. Why Gideon wanted him to do that, though, Charles had no idea.

There was another point, though, which might be a slight source of comfort. The second 'if' in the text message implied that the

stage doorman didn't know that Charles had been in the Duke of
Kent's Theatre the previous evening. Which removed a potential
witness to his presence there. And opened up the possibility that
Charles might get away with his lie.

The reassurance that thought provided didn't last long. He
soon thought of CCTV cameras. The West End was so full of
the bloody things that, even if there weren't dedicated ones
outside the stage door, there was a strong chance that Charles's
movements had been recorded by cameras in the nearby streets.

'How much did you drink last night?' asked Frances.

'A bottle,' Charles mumbled in reply.

'A bottle of wine?'

'Scotch.'

'God. I'm going to come and pick you up.'

'There's no need. I was just ringing to apologize for standing
you up and hurting your feelings yet another time and—'

'This is more important than my feelings. It's your health that's
at risk.'

'Oh, I don't know about that. I've just been bloody stupid and—'

'I'm coming to pick you up.'

It was only after Frances had ended the call that Charles realized
how seriously she was taking the situation. He had phoned her in
the middle of a school day. She had taken the call, even though she
had actually been in a classroom when he got through. And now
she was giving up the rest of her working day to rescue him.

He had expected recriminations as she drove him in her new Skoda
back to Highgate, but her obvious concern made him feel even more
guilty than a serious bawling-out would have done.

When they arrived, Frances decanted him into a hot bath, and
put his previous day's clothes in the washing machine. She brought
a large mug of scalding black coffee and placed it on the rack
across the bath.

Then she fetched the pair of his pyjamas which had been
under the pillow on his side of her bed since the Monday morning.
Even through his pain and discomfort, Charles knew it would be a
long time before he himself ever regained that coveted position. He
was directed to the spare room, made to finish up the coffee, drink
a lot of sparkling water and swallow down two paracetamol.

He didn't know how long he slept, but woke up feeling worse than ever. The shattered, hard components of his brain seemed to have expanded and were now pressing against the interior of his cranium. He felt sick, but in the bathroom once again nothing came up. Just the skeleton-rattling dry retching.

As he wiped his mouth, the mirror showed Frances framed in the open door behind him. 'Get dressed,' she said. 'I've got you a five-forty appointment with the GP.'

'Well, congratulations. I thought these days you had to wait three weeks to get an appointment with your GP.'

'They'll always fit you in,' said Frances, 'when it's an emergency.'

SEVEN

Frances drove him to the surgery, and sat with him in the waiting area. Charles wasn't aware that he was registered with a doctor, but apparently she had kept him on the books of hers. In different circumstances, he might have seen that as an indicator that she considered they had a future together.

He still felt ghastly, but comforted by the fact that Frances had taken over. He knew it was a shameful thing to admit, but he always liked being absolved from responsibility. Maybe that was part of the appeal of his profession. Different for stars, perhaps, but being a jobbing actor is a very passive role, dependent on producers and casting directors to get any work. And, once employed, basically having to do what the director tells you.

That afternoon in the surgery he had no responsibility. He felt like a child again, taken to visit the doctor by his mother.

So, when his name flashed up in red on the screen, it seemed natural for him to ask Frances if she was going to go into the consulting room with him.

'For God's sake, Charles!' she responded. 'In spite of appearances, you are a grown man.'

The doctor, male, had the resigned look of someone who had already decided to take early retirement. And it was the end of a long day. He was looking at the screen of his laptop, presumably checking Charles's details, when his patient entered.

'So,' the doctor said, managing to come up with a smile, 'how can I help you?'

'I'm drinking too much,' Charles confessed.

'Alcohol?'

It hadn't occurred to him that there might be medical conditions that involved drinking too much of anything else. 'Yes,' he replied. 'Alcohol.'

'How much is too much?'

'How do you mean?'

The doctor's hands were busy on his keyboard. 'The latest

government guidelines recommend a maximum of fourteen units a week for both men and women.'

'And what's a unit?' asked Charles blearily.

Again, the doctor had to resort to his screen. Charles felt some level of sympathy. Funny job, not knowing whether the next person through your office door will be talking about terminal cancer, piles or gender reassignment. No time to prepare. Bit like improv for an actor.

The online crib sheet revealed that 'one unit equals 10 ml or 8 g of pure alcohol'.

Charles had to admit he didn't find that very helpful. 'So, how much alcohol would there be in, say, a glass of wine?'

'It would depend on the size of the glass of wine,' said the doctor, in the manner of someone who could think of preferable ways to spend his early evening than doing mental arithmetic. Another look at the screen. 'Well, a pint of strong lager contains three units of alcohol, and a pint of low-strength lager contains two.'

'I don't drink lager. Could you do wine?'

The doctor scrolled down wearily. 'Fourteen units is equivalent to ten small glasses of low-strength wine.'

'Ten? A week?'

'Yes.'

'They are joking, aren't they?'

'I don't think humour is the primary purpose of the NHS Choices website.'

'No, I suppose not.'

The doctor moved a pad of paper to the centre of his desk, and picked up a pen. 'So, Mr Paris, if you could tell me what your daily intake of alcohol is . . .?'

'In units?'

'Tell me in the number of glasses. I'll work out the units.'

'Very well.' And so Charles started to quantify his habit. He had heard somewhere that people telling doctors about their intake of alcohol is one of the most common areas of mendacity in all human activity, so he didn't feel too guilty that his answer probably represented an underestimate.

At the end, the doctor said, 'Hm.' He pressed a key on his laptop. 'Yes, well, you do certainly seem to have a problem, Mr Paris.'

'Maybe. That's just the wine.'

'Sorry?'

'I haven't included the amount of whisky I drink.'

'Ah.' They went through the ritual again. Again, Charles probably underestimated. If the past twenty-four hours had been taken into the calculation, then he certainly would have underestimated.

The doctor produced another jaded 'Hm. Well, you certainly need help.'

'That's why I came to see you, doctor,' said Charles piously. He had kind of erased from his mind that the visit had been Frances's idea.

'Yes, well, obviously we don't run any addiction clinics here at the surgery. Hang on a minute, I'll just check with a colleague who specializes in this area.' And the doctor hurried out of the room.

Charles didn't like the sound of an 'addiction clinic'. It categorized him as a member of a club he had no wish to join.

He looked at the laptop, and felt a strong temptation. He hadn't made many visits to surgeries over the years, but no doubt his records were all there. He rose guiltily from his chair and moved round to look at the screen.

The only word he saw clearly was 'depressive', before the click of the door handle made him shoot back to his seat. He winced. Fast movements were still not a good idea. His brain appeared not to be moving at the same speed as his body, and took a few moments to resettle in his cranium.

The doctor had a selection of printed flyers in his hand. 'Obviously, the best-known organization for your problem is Alcoholics Anonymous.'

'Yes, I have tried that and . . .' God, it was only yesterday. Exactly twenty-four hours before, he'd been sitting in acute discomfort in that Soho church.

'And . . .?'

'And it didn't really work for me,' he understated.

'Oh.' The doctor looked at his watch. There were still more patients in the waiting room who might need his help with terminal cancer, piles or gender reassignment. 'Look, these are some other organizations you can get in touch with. Some are free services, some you have to pay for. I'm afraid we don't have sufficient data to make recommendations as to which you should go with, but I suggest you contact them and—' he handed the sheaf of papers across – 'the ball's in your court.'

As he made his way back to the waiting room, Charles felt mixed emotions. There was a level of disappointment that the doctor hadn't been more impressed by his taking the big step of owning up to a drinking problem. But there was also guilt that he'd been wasting the man's time with what was, ultimately, a self-inflicted illness.

He gave monosyllabic enquiries to the questions Frances asked him as she drove him back to her flat.

'So, did the doctor recommend which clinic you should go to?'

'No.'

'Well, which one did you think sounded best?'

'I haven't had a chance to look yet. I was thinking, when we get back, we could have a look through them and—'

'Not *we*, Charles. You. I've made the appointment and taken you to the doctor. The next steps are over to you.'

'Of course.' He'd somehow hoped Frances would continue her maternal nurturing. As she had done with the surgery, she would make the necessary appointments for him. 'But you will be supporting me?' There was a silence. 'Frances, it was you who said I should do something about my drinking. You got me into this.'

She flared up at that. 'I did not get you into this, Charles! You got yourself into it!'

'Yes, I know, but what I meant was . . . You will help me in my efforts to manage my drinking and—?'

'I will help you in your efforts to *give up* your drinking.'

'That's what I meant.' But he didn't. 'You will support me, though?'

'Yes,' she said. 'From a distance.'

'Are you saying that . . .?'

'From a distance.'

He felt pretty wiped out again by the time he got back to Frances's. 'I think I need to go back to bed.'

She looked rueful. 'All right, you can stay tonight. Presumably, tomorrow you've got to be back in some kind of shape to rehearse, haven't you?'

'I don't know.'

'You said there was no rehearsal today, but presumably everything picks up again tomorrow.'

'There will have been a text from the stage management.'

'Where's your phone?'

'I think it's by the bed in the spare room.'

'Well then, you'd better find it, hadn't you?'

He found it. Needless to say, the battery was flat. 'Oh God, and my charger's back at Hereford Road.'

'I've got a compatible charger,' said Frances.

When his phone was plugged in, he checked the text messages. Half a dozen from Kell Drummond, getting ever more peremptory. Basically, there was to be no *The Habit of Faith* rehearsal on the Wednesday either. There had been a delay on the get-in for the set. And could Charles get back to her to confirm he'd got the message?

Not having received any response to her texts, she had also left a voicemail. Again, could Charles get back to her to confirm he'd got the message?

'I'd better get back to her,' he said to Frances, who was still in the spare room.

'That would seem to be the right thing to do,' she confirmed.

'So, there won't be any rehearsal till Thursday at the earliest.'

'No. You, nonetheless, will be leaving here tomorrow.'

'But, Frances . . .'

She looked at him with a directness that made him avert his eyes. 'Yes? What?'

He gestured to the bed, where lay the flyers he'd been given by the doctor. 'I am going to sort myself out.'

'Good.'

'I'll start ringing round in the morning.'

'From your place.'

'Oh, I thought maybe you might let me—'

'Charles, I thought I made it clear that, for us to cohabit, you were going to have to give up the booze.'

'Yes. I know.'

'Well, you haven't made a very good start, have you?' said Frances, as she sailed out of the room.

Kell answered her phone on the first ring. 'Charles. Where have you been the last twenty-four hours?'

'Oh, round and about.'

'I presume you're finally ringing because you did get my message?'

'Yes, yes, I did. Thank you. Problems with the set fitting into the Duke of Kent's?'

'Exactly.'

'Or at least that's the official line.'

'What do you mean?'

He took a punt, to hide his ignorance. 'Just responding to the rumours going round.'

'Oh yes?' Kell sounded like it wasn't the first time she'd heard something similar.

'Something to do with Liddy Max?' he hazarded.

'I don't know what you're talking about.' But the stage manager's resistance did not last long. 'Oh, there's not much secret about it now, is there? Given the fact that her death's plastered all over the *Evening Standard*. Is that where you saw about it?'

Faced with a choice of lies, Charles said, 'I heard about it from someone in the company.'

'That figures. Not renowned for keeping secrets, actors, are they?'

'No.' Charles moved carefully. He didn't want to give away how much he knew until he knew how much she knew. 'I gather there was a break-in at the theatre last night.'

'Who told you that?'

'The police. A couple of the Boys in Blue – well, not in Blue, actually, plain clothes – came to see me this morning.'

'You too?'

'And you?'

'Oh yes. They've talked to everyone. As if getting a show into a West End theatre wasn't already complicated enough, now we're having our schedule rearranged by the bloody police!'

'So, the set isn't up yet?'

'God, no. And that raises all kinds of other complications. The trucks that were transporting the set can't be left parked in the West End during daylight hours because they block all the traffic and . . . it's a bloody nightmare! Made worse by the fact that there's bugger-all I can do about it. Just sit here twiddling my bloody thumbs.'

'And having the odd drink?' Charles suggested.

'The odd one.' Kell giggled. 'Well, I've been told there's no chance of anything happening till Thursday at the earliest, so in that sense, I can relax a bit, yes.'

'Hm. Do you want any help in your thumb-twiddling and drinking?'

'What are you suggesting, Charles?'

'That maybe you and I could meet up for a drink tomorrow lunchtime.'

There was a silence. Then Kell said, 'I don't see why not.'

EIGHT

Frances had left for school by the time he woke on the Wednesday morning. The night before, she'd given him a Librium, as well as a Zopiclone to help him sleep. 'Where'd you get this stuff from?' he'd asked.

'My emergency detox kit.'

He had looked puzzled. 'Surely not for you?'

'No. Most of the drunks I have to deal with are teenage girls who're not used to alcohol.' Of course. Another of the duties which went with the job of being a headmistress. 'Unlike grown men who should know better.' He was in no position to argue.

She had put a full litre of mineral water by his bedside. 'If you do wake up, just drink as much of this as you can.'

'But if I drink a lot, then I'll wake up again because I need a pee.'

'Excellent. Have the pee, then drink a lot more water. Rehydration is the first thing you need, Charles.'

'Yes.' He had looked at her apologetically. 'I am grateful to you for doing all this, Frances.'

But the only reaction he'd got had been a 'Huh' as she left the room.

He still felt pretty grisly, aching all over, trembling. As he got out of bed the room swayed.

He managed to make it to the kitchen, where he found a note. It had been placed pointedly on top of the pile of flyers he'd got from the doctor, and it read: 'Keep drinking water. Try to eat something, but something bland. There are eggs for scrambling and soup in the fridge. Make sure you phone up those addiction places and begin to sort yourself out. See you some time.'

No 'Love'. But then he didn't deserve love. And, as for the future, just 'some time'. But then he didn't deserve anything more specific.

Charles thought he might be ready to eat something, but just opening the fridge made him want to throw up. The only thing he wanted to pass his lips and stabilize his stomach was a large Bell's.

And, though he knew he mustn't have that, the question did cross his mind as to whether Frances might keep any whisky in the house. He sat down at the kitchen table with his head in his hands.

How had he managed to get himself into this state? Any superiority he might have felt over the other attendees at the Alcoholics Anonymous meeting had by now shrivelled away to nothing. My name is Charles and I am an alcoholic.

He glanced at the flyers on the table. The first one was for a 'Nurse Specialist – Alcohol and Drug Dependence'. He was qualified as an 'RMN' and an 'NMC', whatever those might be. For further details, 'to arrange a consultation or a confidential discussion', there was a phone number to call or the inevitable website to log on to. Charles seemed blurrily to recall that this was one that the doctor had said would cost money. He shuffled it to one side.

The next sheet was offering Clinical Hypnotherapy. Somehow, Charles didn't fancy that, either.

The one that offered him help to Grow and Embrace Life sounded impossibly hippyish.

Group Therapy 'amongst people with similar needs' sounded impossibly chummy.

And the one that offered him a 'Ten-Step Program' was no more appealing. Although there were two fewer steps, it sounded distressingly like Alcoholics Anonymous. And, in the unlikely event of Charles ever wanting a 'Program', then he'd prefer one with a second 'm' and an 'e' on the end. He was distrustful of American psychobabble.

He was surprised by the vehemence of his reaction to every one of the offered solutions.

The sentence that stayed with him from all of this reading was: 'The first step towards recovery is recognizing that you have a problem which you cannot control without outside help.' And Charles wasn't sure that he really had reached that point in his life.

He made himself a large pot of strong coffee, drank most of it, and departed from Frances's house without having rung any of the relevant numbers. What's more, he left all the flyers on her kitchen table.

Going on the tube was a big risk. The chances of Charles actually throwing up in the enclosed space seemed strong. There were plenty of seats, but he felt safer standing up. The motion of the carriage, which normally he would not have noticed, seemed vertiginously violent.

On one of the vacant seats, however, was a copy of the previous day's *Evening Standard*. He picked it up and flicked through the pages with one hand, while the other clung grimly to the ceiling rail. He soon found what he was looking for.

ACTRESS DEATH IN THEATRE
Actress Liddy Max, familiar to viewers of the TV drama Living by Night, *was found dead yesterday in the Duke of Kent's Theatre, where she was soon to open in the play* The Habit of Faith. *She is believed to have had a fall. A police spokesman said that investigations into the cause of her death were continuing.*

There was a uniformed policeman standing outside the stage door of the Duke of Kent's Theatre. As Charles approached, a bright shaft of sunlight suddenly found its way through the roofs around Shaftesbury Avenue, and focused a laser of pain on the area behind his eyes. He winced, then identified himself to the policeman as a member of the cast.

'Didn't you get a message, sir, to the effect that there's no rehearsal today? The building is still under police investigation.'

'Do you mean it's a crime scene?'

'I didn't say that, sir,' the policeman replied stiffly. 'I said that investigations are continuing.'

Charles knew he'd be pushing his luck to ask anything else. 'In fact,' he said, 'I came here because I had a message from the stage doorman. Gideon.'

'Oh yes, I know Gideon, sir. He is actually here, on duty. In case any of the actors needed access to their dressing rooms. Is that what you require, sir, because we'll have to get permission from—?'

'No, no, I just wanted a word with Gideon, if he's around . . .'

'I don't see that's a problem. If it's just something you want to check with him . . .' The policeman moved to open the stage door. 'Gideon! Charles Paris here for you.'

The stage doorman emerged into the opening, blinking like a nocturnal animal in the cold shaft of sunlight. His huge bulk filled the doorway, and there was a scarred bruise in the centre of his forehead.

'I got your text,' said Charles.

'Yes.' Gideon looked indecisive and uneasy.

Charles felt pretty sure that it was the presence of the policeman causing the awkwardness. 'If Gideon and I were to go off for a while, would you have any objection?'

'I can't see a problem with that, sir.'

'Thank you. All right, Gideon? A quick coffee or . . .?'

The stage doorman accepted the offer with alacrity and, as Charles started towards the coffee shop where he'd lunched on the Monday, he was delighted to hear him say, 'No, let's go to the pub.'

Fortunately, the stage doorman's choice of venue was not the one where Charles had fixed to meet Kell an hour later. Somehow, he didn't want to have a gooseberry for that encounter.

Gideon headed for the bar with the sure step of a regular, and though the Eastern European barmaid was early morning bleary, she recognized him. 'Large vodka and T, is it, Gideon?'

'Please. Charles?'

'Oh, I'll just have a fizzy—'

'Thought you were a Scotch drinker.'

'Well—'

'Bell's, didn't I hear?'

'Has been known.'

'No secrets in the theatre,' said Gideon slyly. 'Well, maybe some of us preserve a few, but they're only very secret secrets.' He grinned at Charles, then at the barmaid. 'Make it a large one, Roza.'

'Fine, Gideon.' She looked at Charles. 'Water?'

'Just ice.'

At that hour they were the only customers. Gideon steered the way to a settle, as far from the bar as possible (not that Roza showed any interest in their conversation – or anything else, come to that). They sat in front of a surprisingly convincing fake fire.

Both took long sips from their drinks, as though they were essential medicine. Then Gideon said, 'Glad you came in, Charles.'

'Your text made it sound like we ought to meet. And I heard from Kell about the break-in.' He looked at the bruise, more prominent in the flickering firelight. 'Are you OK?'

'Oh yes. Just a bump.'

'I should mention, Gideon, that I have had a visit from the police.'

The lardy face grew paler. 'You didn't tell them you'd been into the theatre on Monday night?'

'What makes you think I was in the theatre on Monday night?'

'Oh, you weren't there?' Gideon sounded relieved.

Charles trod cautiously. 'I told the police I hadn't been there.'

'Good.'

'What made you think I might have been?'

'The fact that you'd come in in the afternoon. None of the rest of the company had – well, none of the actors, and the techie lot all came in through the scenery dock – but you had come in, and I thought you might already be using your dressing room as, you know, a kind of base in the West End. But if you weren't there, then it's not a problem.'

There was a silence. Both men took long swigs from their glasses. Charles was slightly appalled by how much better he felt with a drink inside him. 'So, about this break-in, Gideon . . .?'

'Ye-es.' Instantly, the stage doorman looked shifty.

'Must've been a shock for you. What actually happened?'

'It was over very quickly. I was in my cubby-hole, actually having a snooze, if the truth were told . . . and suddenly I was aware of someone bursting in and they hit me—' he gestured to his forehead – 'and I think I passed out for a few minutes.'

'Did you see who your attacker was?'

'No, it all happened so quickly.'

'And what time of the evening was this?'

'I don't know exactly. After half-past seven. Like I said, I'd dozed off.'

'And then? Was it you who discovered Liddy's body?'

Gideon nodded. 'But not then. Not straightaway when I come round. Just before midnight, when I was checking the dressing rooms before locking up.'

'I thought the theatre was open for the get-in of the set.'

'Yes, but, like I said, the crew were coming in and out through the scene dock. My orders were to lock up the stage door at twelve.'

'And none of the stage crew saw Liddy's body?'

'They wouldn't, if they were using the scene dock entrance. No reason for them to go near the dressing room stairs.'

'No. Of course not,' said Charles thoughtfully. 'And when you did find her, you called the police?'

'Called Kell first. She got in touch with the producers, then called me back.'

'Had they called the police?'

'No. She told me to. Not much fun, I can tell you, waiting round for them, knowing Liddy was lying there. I was in a bad state.'

'I bet you were.' Charles watched as Gideon drained his glass. The ice clinked as he put it back on the table. 'Get you another of those?'

'Wouldn't say no.'

Charles was pensive as he strolled up to the bar and asked Roza for 'the same again'. When he got back to the table by the fire, he asked, 'And what you've just told me is what you told the police, is it, Gideon?'

'Yes, of course it is.'

'Did they believe you?'

'Why shouldn't they believe me?' He was starting to sound a bit paranoid.

Charles shrugged. 'I don't know. So now they're looking for the bloke who attacked you?'

'I suppose so.'

'Possibly thinking that he was also the one who attacked Liddy?'

'Maybe. I don't know how their minds work, do I?'

'No, you don't.' Charles looked straight at the fat man in front of him. 'And that's what worries you, isn't it?'

'Howdya mean?' The response was defensive.

'I was thinking about that text you sent me, Gideon . . .'

'What about it?'

'Why did you want me to tell the police that I hadn't been into the theatre last night?' No reply, just a shiftier look. 'Was it because you were afraid I might be a witness to what *you* were doing last night?'

'I told you, I wasn't doing nothing. Just sitting in my cubby-hole, maybe dozing a bit.'

'Until you were attacked?'

'Yes, that's right.'

'So you weren't pushing Liddy down the dressing room stairs?'

'No, I bloody wasn't!'

Charles spread his arms wide. 'I didn't think you were, but I had to ask. I wonder what else might you have been doing which you didn't want anyone to witness?'

'Charles it's not important. Since you weren't in the theatre last night, it doesn't matter where I was, does it?'

'Where you *were*? Oh, Gideon, I think I get it.'

'What are you talking about?'

'I think if I had come to the theatre last night, I would have found your cubby-hole empty.' Which of course Charles knew to be true. He had been there, and he had found it empty. But there was no need for him to tell the stage doorman that.

Gideon's body language showed he was on the right track. 'So, where were you?' Charles asked gently.

Too weary to come up with more lies, Gideon replied, 'There's a place some of us go, little cellar round the back of one of the theatres. We drink there. Call it the "Techie's Drinking Club". And I thought last night, there'd be nobody around, just the stage crew, nobody'd notice whether I was on duty or not. God, I'm so bloody stupid!' he burst out. 'I've been off the booze for years, then suddenly I'm back on it. At the classes they keep saying, "Stop mixing with the kind of people who you used to drink with! Keep out of pubs! Keep away from temptation!" And what do I go and bloody do? God, I'm full of shit!'

Charles Paris, looking at the dregs of the morning's second large Bell's, did not feel in any position to comment. 'So, Gideon, you told the police that you were on duty in your cubby-hole all evening?' The fat man nodded miserably. 'And the person who attacked you . . .?'

'No one attacked me,' Gideon confirmed. He gestured to his forehead. 'I did this to myself.'

Kell looked different. At work she always wore black, black jeans or leggings, black T-shirt or jumper, black trainers. Charles did not associate her with colour. And here she was, on a day when she couldn't go to work, dressed in a shiny turquoise zip-top, scarlet jeans and silver lace-up boots.

'I see you've moved away from monochrome,' he said as he approached her.

'Girl's got to be a girl sometimes,' she said, with one of her broad grins.

She had a half-full glass of red wine in front of her.

'Am I late?'

'No, I got here early.'

'More of that?' he gestured to her glass.

'In time.'

Charles really felt like continuing on the Scotch – it was making him feel so much better – but he decided he ought to slow down. 'I'll get a bottle,' he said, feeling speciously virtuous. 'What is that?'

'Malbec.'

'OK.'

This pub was fuller than the previous one. Nearer lunchtime. He had to wait to be served. When he returned to the table, he got another of the grins.

'You'll get yourself a reputation, Charles.'

'What do you mean?'

'Being seen coming from the bar with a full bottle and a single glass. People will talk.'

'No more than they do already.' He unscrewed the top, filled up her glass, then his own, and raised it. 'Cheers!'

'Cheers!' They both took long, grateful swallows, then Kell said, 'Do you want to get the subject of Liddy Max out of the way?'

'I'm in no rush. Be interested to know more about you first.' He put on a slight accent to mitigate the cheesiness of the line. Her smile acknowledged that she knew exactly what he was doing.

'I'm stage manager for *The Habit of Faith*,' she stated without intonation. 'In case you hadn't pieced that together.'

'And?'

'And what?'

He shrugged with hands held open. 'Where do you live? Et cetera?'

'I live in what is described as a studio flat in Crouch End. And, as for the et cetera, I am currently "between relationships". Though the gap since the last one has been so long, "between" may imperceptibly have become "beyond". And you?'

'Oh, technically married, but again it's been a long time since . . .' How readily the lies slipped out. He moved the subject on. 'So, Kell, how did you get into this business?'

'Stage management? Not the usual route. Wasn't a stage-struck teenager. Didn't hope to make it as an actress until I realized the sad truth that I had no talent. No, I went through university, studying computer science. Got roped in to do the lights on some show, through the boyfriend of the moment, who fancied himself as an actor – fancied himself full stop, actually. Anyway, he's long gone.'

'Oh, I am sorry.'

'No, not long gone in that sense. God knows whether he's alive or dead. But he's long gone from my life. Anyway, I found I had

an aptitude for the techie side of theatre, so when I'd got my degree,
I was faced with a choice. A lifetime behind a computer keyboard,
surrounded by other geeks. Or a lifetime dealing with the egos,
freaks and loonies who inhabit "the business that is show".' She
shrugged. 'As you see, I chose the significantly less lucrative route.
Got in on the technical side, lighting, but found that less interesting
once it all became computerized . . . so, ended up in the hole where
you now find me – being blamed for everything by everyone in the
company.'

But she spoke with affection. Clearly, like Charles, though recognizing all the idiocies of the world in which she worked, she was
still bound to it with hoops of iron. Kell took another long pull
from her glass. It would need filling up again soon. 'Incidentally,
Charles, were you planning to eat? It's just . . . I'm ravenous. And
I work on the stage managers' principle of "always eat when you
can, because you never know when the next opportunity will arise".'

Now that the subject of food had been mentioned, he too felt
suddenly starving. Which, considering his reaction when he contemplated the contents of Frances's fridge only a couple of hours earlier,
was amazing. From swearing he would never touch another drop,
he now felt close to eulogizing the beneficial effects of alcohol. It
was with great pleasure that he ordered sausage and mash for both
of them.

'So,' he said when he was back at the table, 'Liddy . . .'

'Yes. Liddy . . .'

'The police came to talk to me at my place, which – like yours
– is a studio flat.'

'Was it the Little and Large of the Met?'

'Mm.'

'They seem to be in charge of the investigation. Detective
Inspector Tricker and Detective Sergeant Bowles.'

'I didn't take in their names. I mean, they introduced themselves,
but . . . Bowles is the short one?' Kell nodded. 'When did you last
speak to them?'

'This morning, actually. They regard me as the person to contact
for any liaison they require with members of the company. Which
is, I suppose, a reasonable definition of the stage manager's role.'

'So, when did Tricker and Bowles first contact you?'

'Small hours of yesterday morning. They told me that Liddy's
body had been found.'

'But you already knew that, didn't you?' She gave him a sharp interrogative look. 'Gideon told me he'd rung you before contacting the police.'

Kell nodded. 'You have been doing your research, haven't you?'

'Just come from having a drink with Gideon.'

'Right. I thought he was meant to be on the wagon.'

'Well, he's fallen off it. When you talked to the cops this morning, did you get any idea of what they were thinking?'

'About Liddy? Whether it was an accident or murder – is that what you mean?'

'I suppose it is, yes.'

Kell grimaced. 'I'm afraid the real police aren't as accommodating as the ones in stage thrillers. They tend not to provide amateur sleuths with regular updates on their investigations.'

'I've heard that.' Charles recalled how helpful and biddable he had been as Detective Inspector Scott in a rather dire play called *Death in the Cocktail Hour*. ('If I ever get murdered, heaven preserve me from having my case investigated by Charles Paris as the Inspector.' *Coventry Observer*.) 'So, you've no idea what they're thinking?'

'Well, from the questions they were asking me, they're still trying to get more information on the intruder who broke into the Duke of Kent's on Monday evening.'

'Suspecting him – or her – of having murdered Liddy?'

She shrugged again. 'Surprise, surprise, they didn't actually volunteer that. But it could be a logical thing to think, couldn't it? I don't know. They'll soon have more information, though. Apparently, they're collecting CCTV footage from the cameras around the stage door area.'

Charles felt a little swoop of despair. That was not what he had wanted to hear. From Gideon's testimony, he now knew the police would find no evidence of any intruder breaking into the theatre. Whereas they would almost definitely find recordings of his own arrival and departure. Realizing he hadn't been telling the truth, they might logically therefore identify him with the intruder. He started to feel paranoid . . . no, that was the wrong word. Paranoia is the fear of non-existent threats. The threat which faced Charles Paris at that moment was very real. Why the hell had he chosen to lie to the police and hope to get away with it?

Anyway, the deed was done. He couldn't retract the statement;

could only wait till his duplicity caught up with him. And, in the meanwhile, he was sitting in a pub, nearing the end of a bottle of wine in the company of a woman whom he was finding increasingly attractive. He kept hearing people saying one should live in the minute, and this was a nice minute to be living in. Particularly since their sausage and mash had just arrived.

'Suppose, Kell,' said Charles, 'that she wasn't killed by an intruder . . .?'

'What, you mean suppose it was an accident?'

'No, let's stay with murder for the time being. Come on, you've sat through endless rehearsals of *The Habit of Faith*. You are the eyes and ears of the production. You see everything that goes on. If you were told that Liddy had been killed by one of the company, in which direction would your suspicions turn?'

'Ooh, accusing company members of murder isn't covered in the stage managers' manual.'

'Just idle speculation . . .?'

'Of the kind that every other person involved with *The Habit of Faith* is currently indulging in?'

'I would say almost definitely yes, Kell.'

'A parlour game?'

'If you like. You must have heard Liddy having a set-to with someone.'

The stage manager wrinkled her lips dubiously. 'Well, if this were a traditional theatrical whodunit . . .'

'Yes?'

'The person we'd be looking for would be Liddy's understudy.'

'Imogen.'

'Right.'

'So, have you witnessed any conflict between the two of them?'

'Not conflict, that would be overstating it, but let's say they weren't bosom buddies.'

'Even though they both came to lunch with us at the sandwich bar on Monday.'

'I think that was just convenience. Leaving the theatre at the same time. Anyway, I haven't actually seen any overt antagonism between the two of them, just no real bonding. But there's no doubt that Imogen's very ambitious. Thinks she's destined to become a star. Any chance of going on for Liddy in a performance, she'd have grabbed it with open arms. In fact, I'll bet she's pretty pleased with the way things have turned out now . . . from her own point of view.'

'Hmm. Thinking back to that *coffee bar lunch* . . .'

'I can tell you didn't enjoy it, Charles.' Kell chuckled. 'Not only from the way you looked while you were eating, but from the way you just said the words.'

He looked around. 'I think somewhere like this is more my natural environment.'

'Mine too, I'm afraid.'

'There's nothing about it to apologize for, Kell.'

'Well, I . . .'

'What do you mean?'

'The fact is, Charles, I have had problems with the booze in the past.'

'Tell me about it,' he said cynically.

'Have been times when it's got out of hand. Now I'm trying to control it. You know, drink properly when I do drink, like today, but have a few days off during the week.'

'And is it working?'

She screwed her face up ruefully. 'To an extent. I think the best I could ever hope to be is a "dry drunk".'

'"Dry drunk"? I don't think I've ever heard that expression.'

'A "dry drunk" is someone who gives up the booze, but doesn't change their mind-set about it.'

'Sorry, that sounds a bit like psychobabble to me.'

'A "dry drunk" still wants to drink. He or she hasn't changed their basic attitude to drinking.'

'Ah. Well, I think I must be one of those. Or probably more of a "wet drunk",' he added facetiously.

'I'm still trying to have my cake and eat it,' said Kell. 'Just cut down on the booze, rather than going for total abstinence.'

'But you suggest that it's working.'

Another wry look. 'I don't know. I backslide a lot. The people at the meetings I go to say I'll have eventually to give it up completely.'

'Meetings? Do you mean AA?'

'No. I have tried that. Didn't work for me.' Charles curbed his instinct to say 'Join the club', as she went on, 'I'm talking about an addiction clinic someone recommended to me. Run by a charity. Called "TAUT".'

' "TAUT" as in teaching?'

'No. "TAUT" as in "T – A – U – T". It stands for something. I can't remember what. Anyway, I don't want to think about that.' She drained her glass 'Today I'm drinking. Today is a drinking day. I will enjoy that while it lasts. When we finally are allowed back into the theatre, I'll be so busy I won't have time to drink.'

'If today's a drinking day,' said Charles, 'then I'd better get the second bottle.' Kell made no demur as he did just that.

'Anyway,' he picked up when their glasses were again full, 'when we had that lunch in the coffee shop, Liddy said she was looking forward to a hot date that evening. I don't suppose you . . .?'

Kell shook her head. 'Don't know anything about her private life . . . beyond the fact that she had a husband with whom she didn't seem to be getting on very well.'

'Derek, yes. You didn't see anyone in the company coming on to her . . .?'

'No more than certain male actors come on to any woman, no.' Charles knew she was referring to their current situation. But she said the words with one of her broad smiles, which took the curse off them.

He grinned in response. 'And Liddy got on all right with Justin, did she?'

'I never witnessed any conflict between them. He seemed happy with the way she was playing The Girl – in other words, exactly as he wanted her to play it.'

This was the first time Charles had heard the stage manager voice anything that might be interpreted as criticism of their star. He responded, 'You mean she was tiptoeing around, not doing anything to upset his performance, like the rest of us?'

'Exactly.'

'You don't know how she came to be cast in *Habit*, do you?'

Kell shook her head. 'Presumably Justin okayed her?'

'I would imagine so. Just wondered if you'd ever heard her mention Bridport?'

'Bridport?'

'As in the town in Dorset, yes.'

Kell looked totally bewildered. 'No, never heard Liddy mention the name. Why do you ask?'

'Doesn't matter. So, anyway, you never saw any conflict between Liddy and any other member of the company?'

'Well, remarkably, she did once have a major set-to with Seamus Milligan.'

'Really? What was it about?'

'It was strange. You know The Girl has that long speech when she describes how she was raped?'

'Yes.'

'Well, she was rehearsing that a couple of weeks ago when—' Kell was interrupted by a ping from her mobile. She found the text and read it quickly. 'Oh God.'

'What is it?'

'Nita. The police have vacated the theatre. We can go back in. There's a planning meeting at three. I must go!'

'But you haven't finished your sausage and mash.'

'Unfinished meals are one of the features of a stage manager's life. Another one is the ability to sober up extremely quickly.'

'And we haven't finished the second bottle of wine.'

'Nita's text says the cast still won't be called till tomorrow morning, so I'll have to leave the second bottle in your capable hands, won't I, Charles?' said Kell, as she rushed out of the pub.

'Well,' he replied to no one. 'If you insist.'

NINE

The hands into which Kell had entrusted the second bottle were less capable by the time Charles had finished it, but he felt quite cheery as he returned to Hereford Road. Although, of course, the immediate target in his emotional life was rapprochement with Frances, spending a couple of hours in a pub with an attractive woman did wonders for any man's self-esteem.

Just as he was entering his studio flat (or 'bedsitter' as he still thought of it), his phone announced the arrival of a text. From Kell. Nothing of a personal nature. A group message, announcing a company call at ten o'clock the following morning. Charles fell on to his bed in a benign stupor, and pulled the duvet over himself.

When he was woken by his phone a couple of hours later, nothing felt benign. Somehow incapable of learning from experience, he'd forgotten how heavy drinking to dissipate a bad hangover provided only temporary respite. The effects were cumulative, and he woke to a new level of shaky ghastliness.

His mood wasn't improved by the fact that the call came from Frances. A very solicitous Frances, concerned about his well-being.

'Yeah, not too bad,' he lied.

'You haven't had anything to drink today, have you?'

'Not much,' he lied again.

'Oh, Charles . . .' The way she said his name expressed decades of exasperation and disappointment.

'Anyway, we rehearse again tomorrow. The police are allowing us back into the theatre.'

'Does that mean they know what happened to the girl who died?'

'If they do, it's not information they're sharing with the general public.'

'No surprise there. So, Charles, have you made an appointment?'

'What?'

'You said you were going to make an appointment with one of those addiction services. The fact that you left all the flyers on the kitchen table made me assume you'd done it.'

'Ah. Well . . .'

'Oh, Charles . . .' Even more exasperation and disappointment.

'I just wanted to get more information,' he faffed around hopelessly. 'Talk to people who've been through the experience, get some recommendations of what's worked for them.'

'And have you got those recommendations?' Frances asked cynically. 'Have you talked to "people who've been through the experience"?'

'Yes, I have, actually,' Charles was able to reply with virtuous honesty. After all, both Gideon and Kell had drink problems, and the stage manager had talked of meetings she went to. 'There's one I'm going to follow up on,' he added, though it was the first time he'd had the idea. 'It's called "TAUT". I'm getting in touch with them tomorrow.'

'Well, make sure you do,' said Frances. 'And don't think about contacting me until you've got an appointment set up.'

He texted Kell. *'Could you give me a number for that TAUT organization you mentioned at lunchtime?'* He hesitated for a moment before concluding the message with an 'X C'.

To his surprise, considering how busy she must be at the Duke of Kent's, she texted him straight back with the number and an address in Finchley, adding, *'I think I'm going to have to get back in touch with them. I feel absolutely shitty. Had I known this was going to be a working day, I wouldn't have dreamed of drinking at lunchtime.'*

No 'X' from Kell.

Charles spent a miserable night. He knew the only thing that would make him feel better was another drink, and he knew the one thing he mustn't have was another drink. Fortunately, there wasn't a bottle of anything alcoholic in the flat, otherwise he would have necked it. And soon it was late enough for all the convenience stores on Westbourne Grove to have closed, so – even if he'd been tempted to succumb – he had no source of supplies.

As a result, he sweated through the small hours, snatching moments of sleep and waking either too hot or too cold. Round three o'clock, he took his last two paracetamol, and wished he possessed something in the way of sleeping pills. Round six, he gave up the unequal struggle and risked moving his head into vertical.

He drank a lot of strong coffee and tap water, but they made a poor job of rehydrating his arid brain.

'It is a hell of a tight schedule, but I think the show's in pretty good shape and we can make it in time for the Press Night.'

Nita Glaze was speaking, but everyone in the auditorium that Thursday morning knew that she was channelling the thoughts of the show's producers and star. Nita had the title of director, but those kinds of decisions were way above her pay grade. She had been given the illusion of power, though. Justin Grover and the producers sat meekly in the stalls, while she was alone on stage, delivering their pronouncements.

'Obviously,' she went on, 'we're all shattered by what happened to Liddy, and it's not going to be easy to bring our focus back on to *The Habit of Faith*. But we're all professionals, and there's nothing she would have wanted more than for us to do the show as well as we possibly can, as a kind of tribute to her memory.

'As you can see . . .' she gestured round to the incomplete set 'there's a lot of work still to be done here and, though from now on, we are nominally rehearsing in the theatre, there may be times when major structural work means we have to go elsewhere. Because of the time pressure, we won't be going back to White City, but, Kell, I think you're on the case for finding some rehearsal space in the West End . . .?'

From the auditorium, the stage manager nodded assent. 'Getting there,' she said.

Apart from a generic greeting to the company, Kell hadn't spoken directly to Charles that morning. She looked pale and drawn. It was quite possible that, monitoring the stage crew's set-building overnight, she hadn't had any sleep. And starting on that kind of workload with a skinful of booze can't have helped. Maybe she was avoiding Charles's eye, because she blamed him for leading her astray.

Or maybe he was just being paranoid, another uncomfortable feeling to add to the collision of uncomfortable feelings occupying his mind and body. He sat in the front row, sweating and jerky, wishing he'd equipped himself with a cup of coffee like most of the company, but uncertain whether he'd be able to get it to his lips without spillage.

*   *   *

Charles was not involved in the first scenes being rehearsed that morning, so he ambled disconsolately up to his dressing room. His was up two flights of the steep stairs. Liddy's, now the domain of Imogen Whittaker, was on the first floor, so he passed the landing from which she had fallen, been propelled, or propelled herself on the Monday evening.

Being back there made him wonder again what conclusions the police had arrived at from their investigations. Despite any amount of backstage speculation, it was unlikely that any definitive information would emerge until the poor girl's inquest. And questions like why on earth she had been dressed in one of the monk's habits might not even be answered then.

Charles's dressing room depressed him. The prospect of having his own private niche for three months in the West End had already palled. He knew it was his own fault. His Monday night tryst with a bottle of Bell's had sullied the place for him.

He also felt guilty about Liddy. If he hadn't been insensible with drink, he might have heard something which could have given a clue as to what had happened to her. He might even, possibly, have been able to save her life.

The only thing that had stopped him from doing that was the drink. Nothing else. And the reason he was feeling so shitty that morning had the same cause. It was also the reason why he was about to screw up the most promising rapprochement with his wife that he'd been offered for years. My name's Charles and I am an alcoholic.

Kell's text was still on his phone. TAUT. He wondered what the acronym stood for. But that wasn't important. He rang the number.

A female voice answered, calm, slight London twang, just with the word, 'TAUT.'

'Good morning. A friend recommended that I should ring you.'

'Good. And may I ask what your problem is?'

He felt flustered. 'What do you mean?'

'Here at TAUT we deal with a variety of addictions. Drugs, alcohol, gambl—'

'I've never taken drugs,' said Charles piously, almost perversely affronted that the suggestion should be made. (His lack of experience of illegal substances was not due to some high moral decision to abstain. It was just that, when in his late teens a friend had offered him a spliff and he had taken a couple of long drags, all he got from the experience was a headache so agonizing that he had forsworn drugs ever since. From that time on, he'd never smoked cigarettes either. As an embryonic actor, he already knew how useful it was to have something to do with one's hands, but while his schoolfriends looked cool going through the elaborate routines of the smoker, Charles kept picking bits of tobacco off his tongue, and generally was more adolescently inept with a cigarette than without one. Thus, concern with external appearances had protected him from two health-threatening habits. If only the same could have been said of the booze.)

'So, what is the problem?' came the question from the other end of the line.

'Alcohol,' he managed to say.

'Fine.' The voice was completely unjudgemental. 'What I would suggest is that we should make an appointment for you to come here for an assessment, and then we'll see where we go from there.'

'That sounds a good idea.'

'I've got nothing till the week after next. Is Monday a possibility?'

'Should be all right. I'm in a show which will have opened by then.'

'Ah. You're "in the business"?'

'Yes.'

'Well, let's say four o'clock Monday week.'

'Thank you. Of course, if I'm called for extra rehearsals, I'll—'

'Just give us a call and we'll reschedule.'

'Fine.'

'Reckon the assessment will take an hour.'

'OK.'

'Right. Your meeting will be with Erica. Do you have our address?'

'Yes. "Gower House" was it?'

'That's right.' She gave him some directions. 'If I could just have your name and mobile number . . .'

The warm feeling from having done the deed didn't last long. He still felt shitty, and with that came the sour reflection that the shittiness was completely self-imposed.

He contemplated ringing Frances to tell her he'd taken the first step, that he had actually made the appointment. But he decided against it. Wait until he had some progress to report.

He folded his *Times* to the crossword page, but the clues appeared to be written in a foreign language. Though it was their business to make connections between ideas, all the synapses in his brain had gone on strike.

The only thought that his mind seemed able to accommodate was a disquieting one. Kell had told him the police were checking CCTV footage for the Monday night. It was only a matter of time before they would be wanting to ask him more questions. He regretted his total stupidity in lying to them in the first place.

Charles wandered disconsolately down to the Green Room and made himself a mug of coffee (which he only filled up halfway to avoid tremor spilling). Then he went into the auditorium to see what was happening in rehearsal.

They were working on The Girl's big scene, in which she described to Abbot Ambrose the violence that had brought her to seek sanctuary in the monastery. The company referred to it as 'The Rape Scene', and it was the one over which Nita Glaze and Liddy Max had clashed. But the atmosphere was patently more relaxed with the new casting.

It was also immediately clear that Imogen Whittaker was a very good actress. With her long red hair and her stunning looks, she had quite a future ahead of her. She had also done her homework. Only three days after she had been told she was playing the part, she knew every one of The Girl's lines perfectly. (This is of course what she should have been able to do as the cover for Liddy Max, but very few understudies are as familiar with the text at that stage of rehearsals.)

The standard of Imogen's performance also suggested that in the intervening couple of days, she had either been working very hard on the part on her own, or with Nita's guidance. Charles supposed there was no reason why the two of them shouldn't have got together in a rehearsal room while access to the Duke of Kent's was barred.

He thought idly of the eternal cliché of showbiz mysteries – the star being got out of the way so that the understudy can blossom into an even bigger star – and wondered whether it had any relevance to the current situation. He couldn't really see it.

There weren't many of the company in the auditorium that meeting. Nita, her assistant director, a couple of ASMs. No sign of

Kell; maybe she was on the phone, sorting out alternative rehearsal space.

The other person present, though, was Seamus Milligan. He was watching his lines being delivered with rapt attention. And the looks he focused on Imogen Whittaker were so intense as almost to be hungry.

TEN

B y a remarkable combination of team effort, hard work and a great deal more expensive overtime than the producers would have wished for, *The Habit of Faith* did open for its Press Night on schedule. And, though there had been fewer previews than originally planned, the show wasn't in bad shape. Obviously, Justin Grover gave the performance that he had fixed in place before rehearsals even started, but the rest of the cast matched up to his proficiency. And, technically, there were no hitches. Though Nita Glaze had not had as much artistic input as she might have wished, she demonstrated impressive skill in the logistical challenge of getting a West End show to open on time.

And *The Habit of Faith* got ecstatic reaction from its Press Night audience. The usual mix of investors, critics, friends of the cast and B-list celebrities was on this occasion enriched – or impoverished, according to your point of view – by a substantial contingent of people dressed as characters from *Vandals and Visigoths*. They ensured that, when Abbot Ambrose unveiled himself at the end of the opening line-up, yes, he did get his anticipated round of applause.

There were at least a dozen Sigismund the Strongs in the audience, and a couple of versions of his son Wulf, but Skelegators easily won the numbers game. And, of course, there were a lot of teenage girls, who squealed at every appearance of Grant Yeoell. The fans were surprisingly well behaved, hiding any disappointment that they might have felt about *The Habit of Faith* diverging considerably from the movie plotlines they were anticipating. But they did look funny queuing at the bar in the interval.

The evening was all about Justin Grover, of course, but he was very skilled at the art of apparent self-depreciation. After his first solo curtain call, he urgently summoned the rest of the cast back on stage, as if to say, 'I couldn't have done it without them.' Whereas, the cynical thought occurred to Charles as he joined in the practised bows, Justin would have preferred to have done it without anyone.

At one point, the star raised a hand to still the audience's noisy appreciation and, turning appropriately sober-faced, announced, 'Of course, there is one person who is sadly not with us tonight . . .'

He proceeded to give a graciously worded encomium to Liddy
Max, concluding that all the company had endorsed his suggestion
of dedicating the evening's performance to her memory. This statement was greeted by renewed, and even more vigorous, applause.

In his few words, Justin Grover also praised the speed and skill
with which Imogen Whittaker had stepped into the breach at such
short notice. He even went as far as to say that those watching her
performance as The Girl that evening 'are witnessing the birth of
a major theatrical talent'.

Looking along the line of cast drawn up behind their star, Charles
could see Imogen glowing in the spotlight of attention. It was true,
though, what Justin Grover had said. The young actress had risen
magnificently to the challenge of the Press Night and her performance was way better than anything she had produced in rehearsal.

If this evening did prove to be the breakthrough to stardom for
Imogen Whittaker, Charles knew he would always feel a flicker of
disquiet about the circumstances that had led to her becoming The
Girl. There were still many questions about Liddy's death that
remained unanswered.

As Justin Grover stepped back into the line of actors, 'among
whom', as he constantly repeated, 'he was just another member of
the ensemble', the clapping recommenced. And where the light from
the stage spilled on to the front row, he saw the theatre-goers rising
to give *The Habit of Faith* a standing ovation.

Frances wasn't present. A West End Press Night was a rare enough
occurrence for Charles Paris, and he had invited her to come. He'd
even suggested extending the invitation to Juliet and Miles – give the
son-in-law something about Pops to be proud of – but Frances had
said she didn't want to see him 'until you've sorted yourself out'.

A lot of the old London theatres have unexpected spaces hidden
away in their upper reaches, and it was in one of these, a private
meeting room, in which the post-Press Night drinks were organized.
There was genuine champagne – *The Habit of Faith* producers were
not the kind to fob their employees off with prosecco – and large
plates of sandwiches, on which the actors fell like vultures. As actors
always do. Maybe it's the long tradition of precariousness in their
profession which makes them always hoover up any food that's on
offer.

None of the actors had elaborate costumes to remove – one of the advantages of monks' habits – but Charles still managed to be first upstairs for the drinks. He took a glass of champagne from the rows on a table. The only other person in the room was tall, gloomy and drinking Perrier. 'Hello. I'm Charles Paris.'

'Yes, I saw you in the show.'

Charles waited, in the actor's eternal hope of commendation, but none came, so he said, 'Ah. And what's your involvement?'

'I'm an investor.'

'Right.' Charles chuckled. 'On the side of the angels.' The glazed expression he received suggested that the investor didn't know that people of his kind were nicknamed 'angels'. 'You didn't give me your name,' Charles went on.

'No, I didn't,' the investor agreed.

Further conversation was fortunately interrupted by the arrival of other cast members. At such Press Night occasions there is always an exuberance, a communal relief at finally having got the show opened. But tonight's euphoria seemed less manic and fragile than was often the case. Even if they hadn't known that Justin Grover's name on the marquee had ensured their three-months' stay in the West End, there was a confident feeling that the evening's performance had gone well. With an audience there, *The Habit of Faith* had really opened out. Even Charles Paris was wondering whether his assessment of 'a seriously crap play' may have been a little hasty.

When everyone was assembled, the producers said a few words of congratulation to the company. And then Justin Grover added a few humble words of his own, saying what a privilege it had been to be part of such 'a dedicated ensemble'.

And then those present who were drinking had a few more drinks.

Charles was surprised – and slightly disappointed – to see how many weren't drinking. He knew they all had a matinee and an evening show to do the next day, but what kind of actor didn't have a drink after a Press Night? Surely even teetotallers should relax their principles for such a special occasion?

Justin Grover, having raised his champagne glass to the rest of the ensemble and taken a modest sip, had then put it to one side and moved on to Perrier. But that was maybe to be expected. In the days of mobile phone cameras and social media, he could not ever put his star status at risk by getting drunk.

However much they wished it did, that didn't apply to the rest of the company. None of them was famous enough for anyone to care whether they got drunk or not. And yet a scary number of them seemed to have joined the Perrier party.

Kell, Charles noticed, had a glass of fizzy water. He went across and, perhaps to assert his own virtuousness, said, 'I've followed up with TAUT. Going to have an assessment next week. With someone called Erica.'

'She's good. Well, they're all good.' Kell didn't seem to be focusing on him; her eyes were flitting round the room.

'Are you likely to be going there?' asked Charles, quite relishing having Kell's company for the next stage of his journey to sobriety.

'I hope not.'

'Oh?' He was taken aback by the sharpness of her tone.

'Sorry, that came out wrong. I didn't mean to knock what they do at TAUT. It's brilliant. I just meant I hope I'll be able to get through this next patch from my own inner resources.'

'Ah. Well, good luck.'

'Thanks. Oh, there you are,' she said, breaking away from Charles and taking the arm of Tod Singer, who had just arrived.

Charles went to get his champagne glass filled up.

He still had a headache when he arrived at the Duke of Kent's on the Wednesday afternoon. He was there a good hour before the matinee, clutching a virtuous sandwich he'd bought from one of the Hereford Road convenience stores. Not going to give in to the temptation of a pub lunch.

Because he was early, there were not many other company members about, which provided a welcome opportunity to talk to Gideon on his own.

'All the fuss about Liddy seems to have died down a bit,' he observed. 'Everyone's been so busy getting the show on.'

Gideon nodded, starting a ripple through the rolls of flesh where his neck should have been.

'You had any more hassle from the police?' Charles went on casually.

'They did talk to me this morning.'

'And? Have they made up their minds about what actually happened to Liddy?'

'Well, if they have, they didn't tell me. Been in touch with you again, have they?'

Gideon's question seemed to imply some level of complicity

between the two of them. As if they both had something to hide about the night Liddy died. Gideon's secret was the fact that he'd been off drinking when he should have been on duty. Charles felt confident that the stage doorman didn't know what his was.

'No. Haven't heard a squeak. Maybe they've decided it was an accident. Or maybe it'll be one of those cases where they can never find out the truth about what actually happened.'

'Maybe.' But there was still important information Charles needed from Gideon. Maintaining the casual tone, he said, 'I heard from someone that the cops were going to check out the CCTV footage from round this area . . . you know, on the relevant night. You hear anything from them about that?'

Gideon's chubby face crinkled into a smile. 'Yes, I did. And thank the Lord, it was good news.'

'Oh?'

'Seems that all the CCTV cameras in the area had been sabotaged. Paint sprayed all over the lenses.'

'When was it done?'

'No idea. Cops didn't tell me that. But, like I say, it's good news for me. It's evidence that the raid was planned.'

'What raid?'

'The raid by the intruder who hit me over the head.'

'But you told me there never was an intruder who hit you over the head.'

'You know that, I know that.' The stage doorman winked conspiratorially. 'But the police don't know that, do they?'

Their conversation was interrupted by the arrival at the stage door of one of the wardrobe girls.

'Anyway, Charles,' said Gideon, 'if you fancy going for a drink after the show one night, I'd be up for it.'

'Me too,' said Charles, convincing himself he was agreeing, not because he fancied a drink, but because he wanted to pick Gideon's brains further about the mystery of Liddy Max's death.

As he walked up the steep stairs to his dressing room, Charles Paris felt enormous relief. There was no CCTV footage to prove that he'd lied to the police about his movements on the relevant night. He had got away with it.

To Charles's amazement, *The Habit of Faith* got very good reviews, most of them concentrating on Justin Grover's performance. What

versatility he had, moving from the craggy grandeur of Sigismund
the Strong to the fragile sensitivity of Abbot Ambrose! How splendid
it was that an international movie star had returned to work onstage
in the West End!

And, to Charles's disappointment, none of the reviews mentioned
what a piece of crap the play was. So, what did he know?

None of the reviews mentioned him either. But then he'd known
from the start that he was only in the play as a plot device, a listener
to what were effectively monologues from all the other characters.

Anyway, he wasn't too upset. He remembered the last review
he's received when he'd played a part in a monk's habit. ('In the
role of the prior, Charles Paris's bellicose ranting made me wish
he'd joined a Trappist order.' *Bolton Evening News*)

'Frances, it's Charles.'

It was the Friday, just before the show opened. End of a busy
school week for her.

'Oh yes?' There was no intonation in her words, neither
welcoming nor deterrent. 'Press notices for your show seemed to
be pretty good.'

'They were, weren't they? You must come and see it sometime
when we've—'

'Yes.' She didn't sound particularly enthusiastic. 'Listen, Charles,
I'm about to luxuriate with a glass of wine in the long hot bath I've
been promising myself all week, so if you just rang to pass the time
of day, then I'd—'

'No, no. I did have a reason for ringing.'

'And what was that?'

'I wanted to tell you, I have been in touch with TAUT.'

'TAUT? What's that?'

'It's a charity which helps people with addiction problems.'

'Oh, good, Charles.' Her tone was instantly softer. 'I thought
you'd conveniently forgotten our discussions about that.'

'No. I was just waiting till we got the show opened. I'm going
to TAUT to have an assessment on Monday.'

'Good. It's a start. And may I ask . . . have you had a drink
today?'

'No,' Charles replied proudly.

'Yet,' said Frances, with the weariness of many years' experience.

He didn't respond to that. 'Anyway, I was thinking . . .'

'Mm?'

'Because I have taken the first step, you know, setting up this assessment interview—'

'Yes?' She sounded as if the imperative of her bath was growing stronger with every second.

'I wondered if we could meet up on Sunday night, at the Italian place . . .?'

'And will you turn up this time? I've had my fill of looks from other diners, pitying The Woman Whose Date Didn't Turn Up.'

'No, I'll be there, I promise. Go on, please say yes.'

Frances let out a long sigh. 'All right, Charles, I'll meet you there . . . on one condition.'

'What's that?'

'That you make me another promise.'

'Mm,' he said warily.

'Not to have a drink between now and then.'

There was a silence, then, 'All right, I'll do it.'

'See you Sunday,' said Frances. 'Perhaps.'

He was there at the Hampstead place on the Sunday. And he hadn't had a drink since they spoke on the phone.

Nor, to the amazement of the waiters, who knew the couple well, did he order anything alcoholic. As he watched his wife down two large Cabernet Sauvignons, Charles Paris sipped San Pellegrino.

He felt virtuous, but knew the evening would have gone better if he had been drinking. There were pauses and longueurs in their dialogue, which he was sure he wouldn't have been aware of with a drink inside him. Frances seemed tired, and Charles, listening to the lively banter from the tables around them, felt old.

When he paid the bill, there was no thought of Frances inviting him back to her place. She asked him to report back to her on his assessment at TAUT, kissed him on the cheek and left.

Charles returned disconsolately on the tube to Queensway, warmed only by the knowledge that he had a barely opened litre of Bell's waiting for him back at the flat.

ELEVEN

When he arrived at Gower House, he had been surprised at its grandeur. A tall Victorian villa in Finchley, whose value, given London's rocketing prices, must have been in multiple millions. Whether the whole house was given over to TAUT, he had no means of knowing. The waiting room to which he had been directed was white-emulsioned and functional. There was a small stainless-steel sink in the corner, and next to it a surface littered with mugs, kettles, boxes of tea bags and industrial-sized tins of instant coffee. On corkboards on the walls were flyers about addiction support from the NHS and other, less official, organizations. One wall was painted with a not-very-good mural of a faceless man breaking free from heavy chains.

As he entered, a smiling man was making himself a mug of tea. 'You want a hot drink?' he offered cheerily.

'No, thanks. Just had some coffee,' Charles lied.

'Well, take a seat.'

The man volunteered his name, but Charles didn't know whether he was on the staff or one of the . . . what was the right word? Patients? Customers? Addicts?

'All first names here,' the man said, and introduced the two other seated men. They looked relaxed. This was clearly a venue they knew well. The only female in the room, an unhealthily thin girl who had the shakes, said nothing.

'I'm Charles,' he responded, cutting off the insane impulse to add, 'and I'm an alcoholic.'

'So how much would you say you are drinking, Charles?'

'Well, if you count the last few days, very little.' He conveniently forgot the couple of large glasses of Bell's he had downed when he got back to Hereford Road the previous evening.

'But presumably that's not typical, or you wouldn't have got in touch with us?'

Erica was probably ten years younger than Charles. A thickset woman with dark-rimmed glasses and black hair caught up with a rubber band into a kind of untidy topknot. No wedding ring, jeans and a purple fleece. She wore no make-up, and her face looked as if it wasn't used to smiling. But maybe that was just a mask she wore professionally. The problems she was dealing with were, Charles imagined, rarely funny.

She had a pad of paper on the table between them, and was making notes on Charles's answers. 'So how much do you usually drink, Charles?'

'Are you talking in units, like government health guidelines?'

'I'm not too worried about those. Tell me in terms of glasses per day. Or bottles, if that's more appropriate.' Still no hint of a smile, accompanying what some people might have considered a joke.

'Well, it depends really on what's happening in my life.'

'You're an actor, you say?'

'Yes. I've just opened in a show in the West End.' She showed no interest in what that show might be. 'So, the pattern's different when I'm actually in work.'

'And actors do spend quite a lot of time out of work, I believe.'

'It depends what kind of actor you are. *I* spend quite a lot of time out of work.'

'Do you drink more, or less, when you're out of work?'

'Hard to say. More likely to drink during the day when you're out of work. And being out of work is depressing, so you drink more then, anyway.'

'You know that alcohol is a depressant?'

'I've heard it said, yes.' Charles's mental jury was out on that one. When he woke in the middle of the night after a skinful, he often felt depressed. But the way his gloom lifted after a couple of drinks generally seemed to make the indulgence worthwhile.

He went on, 'If you've got a show to do in the evening, the idea is that you don't have a drink until after you've finished.' He knew that 'the idea is' was a rather feeble expression, which didn't really define his drinking habits.

'So, back to my question about how many glasses – or bottles – you drink . . .?'

'Well, I suppose . . . half a bottle of wine most days.'

'Beer?'

'Occasionally.'

'Spirits?'

'I enjoy the odd glass of whisky.'

'How often?'

'Most days,' he conceded.

'Just the one glass?'

'Well, sometimes more.'

'So, in the average week . . .?' Erica's pen hovered over her pad. Though they weren't actually printed on the page, there were boxes she needed to fill.

'Ooh, let's say . . . over the week . . . three bottles of wine, a couple of pints of beer and . . . maybe half a bottle of Scotch?' It was a considerable underestimate. But presumably, in her job, she was used to that.

'And when was the last day you didn't have any kind of alcoholic drink?'

'Yesterday,' he replied virtuously, then had to correct himself to 'Saturday.'

'Before that?'

'Friday.'

'And before that?'

'Ah.' His memory couldn't cope with that one.

'Going back to your wife . . .'

'Yes.'

'Have you become violent towards her?'

'Good Lord, no. I'm not one of those drunks who gets aggressive. I get silly first, then more, sort of, pathetic and self-pitying.'

'But you say your wife encouraged you to get help?'

'Yes. We don't actually live together.'

'Oh?'

'Both got our own places. Have done for . . . I don't know how many years. Over twenty, anyway.'

Erica's pen moved quickly across the pad as she noted down these details. 'But she still clearly takes an interest in your life . . . or in your health, anyway?'

'Yes.'

'So, was there some particular incident which made you get in touch with us?'

'What kind of incident?'

'Were you arrested for drunken behaviour? Did you cause an accident through driving when drunk? Did you pass out and have no recollection of a certain period of time?'

'No, none of those things.' Charles thought about the questions for a moment, and remembered the night of Liddy Max's death. 'Well, there have sometimes been evenings when I kind of . . . can't remember what happened.'

'Recently?'

'There was a bad one the Monday before last.'

Erica made a note. 'And it was after that that your wife recommended that you seek help?'

'No. She suggested it before that happened. I mean, actually she's suggested it many times over the years.'

'And have you ever followed her advice?'

'Sorry?'

'Have you tried other forms of therapy? I ask these questions so that I can get a background to your history of addiction. It helps us to know the best ongoing treatment for you.' Charles didn't really like the word 'treatment'. It sounded horribly medical. 'I mean, for instance, it would help us to know if you've ever tried Alcoholics Anonymous.'

'I did once go to a meeting, with a friend.'

'When was this?'

It felt like an age ago, though his reply was: 'Last week.'

'And how did you feel about the AA programme?'

'I loathed it. It made me very cross.' In fact, he thought but didn't say, 'It was in reaction to that meeting that I went off on the worst bender I've been on for years.'

'AA doesn't suit everyone,' said Erica, in a tone that was studiedly non-judgemental. 'Another question I should ask . . . Have you ever woken up in the morning with such a hangover that you needed another drink before you could get on with your day?'

Charles admitted that that had happened. 'But not very often.'

Again, Erica made no comment or judgement. 'Going back to your wife, why suddenly now have you followed her advice, to get treatment?'

'She raised the possibility of our living together again.'

'And is that something you would like to happen?'

Charles found the direct question difficult. 'Yes. I mean, obviously it would be a big commitment, but . . . Well, yes, I think so.'

Their session ended within the hour. Erica was clearly a skilled practitioner who had done this kind of interview many times before.

She explained to Charles that TAUT was a charity, which currently had no government funding. Its sessions were free to any clients who sought them out or were referred by other bodies. They had no residential facilities, but were in touch with other organizations should hospitalization become necessary. In the same way, while there were no doctors in the building, they were in regular contact with medical practitioners, should their services be required.

The only rules on which TAUT insisted were that no drugs or alcohol were allowed on the premises, and that a rule of confidentiality was observed about anything that was said in any of their sessions.

At the end of the assessment, Erica gave Charles two photocopied sheets. On the 'Drink Diary' he should enter his daily intake of alcohol and put answers in columns headed 'Did You Drink?', 'What Did You Drink?' and 'How Do You Feel Now?' On the 'Reduction Plan', he was meant to list his 'Current Amount', the amount he intended to reduce that by and the 'Amount Achieved'. Charles somehow couldn't see himself doing all that paperwork every time he reached for the Bell's bottle.

Erica also gave him a sheet listing the weekly timetable at Gower House. There was a very full programme, with sessions of an hour or hour and a half continuing between ten a.m. and eight p.m. every weekday. The titles of these sessions contained a lot of off-putting words like 'Community', 'Grounding' and 'Development'.

Her recommendation for Charles was that he should try the 'Growing Out' meeting at noon on Thursdays and see how he got on with it. If that proved to be useful, then perhaps he should consider attending the 'Weekend Group' on Fridays at four in the afternoon. For a lot of the participants, Erica explained, the weekend was the most dangerous time, when the temptations of social alcohol and substance abuse were at their strongest. The Friday sessions were more free-form than the others. Though they were led by a member of the TAUT staff, he or she tended to sit back and let the participants guide their own discussion.

Charles was interested by her careful use of words. Like 'participant'. Other possibilities that occurred to him were 'addict', or even 'patient'. But no, the people attending the TAUT programme were 'participants'. Though Charles had a natural scepticism about woolly New Age concepts like 'sharing', he respected the use of the word.

In spite of himself, on the tube back into Central London, he was intrigued. And in his meeting with Erica there had not been a whiff of the religiosity which had so put him off Alcoholics Anonymous.

He also wondered again what the acronym 'TAUT' stood for.

Though cynical about his chances of changing the habits of a lifetime, at least he was prepared to take the next step.

When he went in through the stage door, Gideon pointed out to him an envelope tucked into the lattice of ribbon on the corkboard for the cast's mail.

'Thank you,' said Charles, taking it.

'And we'll have that drink after the show one night?'

'Sure.'

'I could do this evening.'

'Erm . . . No, something I've got to do this evening,' Charles lied. He probably would want to pick Gideon's brains again at some point, but his visit to Gower House was too recent. He remembered something Erica had said about 'avoiding situations that lead to drinking'.

At the top landing, he looked along to what had been Liddy Max's dressing room. Now Imogen Whittaker's. The understudy had had no qualms about taking it over. She wasn't spooked by using a dead woman's dressing room. Now she'd got the part of The Girl, she wanted all the benefits that came with the job.

As he had this thought, Imogen herself came hurrying out. 'Oh, hi, Charles. Just going out to get a sandwich for later. See you.' And she scampered off down the stairs.

He had no control, as his feet took him ineluctably into the dressing room.

What surprised him was how familiar it was. Though the make-up laid out in front of the mirror was Imogen's, though the good-luck cards Blu-Tacked on to the mirror were Imogen's, the room still felt exactly as it had when Liddy was in residence.

But how did he know that? Charles had no recollection of ever going into Liddy Max's dressing room. He would have had no reason to. He'd often dropped into the dressing rooms of other male cast members for a bit of pre-show banter, but he hadn't known Liddy that well. And when he'd met her on the landing the day she died, he'd seen her go towards the door with her key at the ready, but he'd been off down the stairs before she'd opened it.

He looked around the room. Yes, he had been there before. He recognized the old moulded plasterwork, its outlines smoothed away by many coats of paint. The most recent colour was a deep apricot. He recognized the vertical pipes in the corner of the room, again much painted, something to do with the theatre's deeply inefficient heating system. He moved closer to them. There were tenacious blobs of Blu-Tack and a shred of painted-over gaffer tape on the pipes, no doubt fixatives for the First Night cards of a previous occupant.

He heard footsteps coming up the stairs and moved out, on the way to his own dressing room.

And as he mounted the second flight of stairs, he realized that the only time he could have gone into Liddy Max's dressing room was during the evening of her death, the night whose details had been obliterated from his memory by Bell's whisky.

He sat down in front of his mirror, and tried to focus, but further details remained elusive. All he knew was that he had been into Liddy's dressing room that night.

Why he went there, and what he did there, were questions that remained resolutely unanswered. It was very frustrating. But the door to those memories had opened a tiny crack. Perhaps in time more recollection would come to him.

He realized that he hadn't opened the envelope he'd picked up at the stage door. It was hand-written.

> *Dear Charles,*
> *I am Liddy Max's husband and I'm trying to establish the circumstances of her death. The police will tell me nothing, so I am contacting other people who might be able to shed some light on the tragedy. Please contact me by phone or email. I am desperate to find out what happened.*
> *Derek Litwood*

Charles rang the mobile. He fixed to meet the young widower the next day at the Patisserie Valerie near the Duke of Kent's. Five o'clock, before Tuesday evening's performance.

The note he had been left was interesting, but also slightly unnerving. Charles's had been the only envelope on the stage door corkboard, which suggested that Derek Litwood had not made a blanket appeal to all the cast. So why had he picked on Charles

Paris as a source of information? Did that mean he knew Charles had been in the theatre on the night in question?

The possibility was troubling. As was the tiny glimmer of recollection he had had in Liddy Max's dressing room, suggesting as it did that he might in time recover the memory of the whole evening.

And what revelations would that bring? Was it possible that Charles had been in some kind of alcohol-induced fugue state? That he could have behaved in a manner that was completely out of character?

Was it possible, at the worst, that it was he who had pushed Liddy Max to her death?

He cursed the inadequacy of his memory. And he cursed the alcohol that caused that inadequacy.

TWELVE

Derek Litwood was as smartly and conventionally dressed as he had been when Charles saw him out of the coffee shop window the Monday before. He established very quickly that he was a solicitor by profession, and that he had been given compassionate leave from work since his wife's death.

'Though, in fact,' he said, 'I'm not so much grieving as furiously angry. I want to know the truth about how Liddy died, and all I encounter is obstruction.'

'Obstruction from the police?' asked Charles.

'Obstruction from everyone, but yes, mostly from the police. They're obviously deep into their own investigations, but they won't give me any information. I've still no idea whether they reckon her death was an accident, or something more sinister. So, as I said in my note, I'm desperate to talk to anyone who can shed any light on what really happened.'

Charles knew he had to be cautious. Unless Derek Litwood had actually witnessed his presence at the Duke of Kent's that night, he would stick to the story he had told the police. That he hadn't been there. That he hadn't seen Liddy's broken body at the foot of the stairs.

'I'm very happy to tell you anything I know,' he said carefully, 'but I'm afraid that doesn't amount to very much.'

'Well, the first thing I should make clear,' said Derek, 'is that my marriage to Liddy was going through a rough patch.'

Charles had got that impression from the scene he'd witnessed outside the coffee shop, but he made no comment.

'The fact is, her getting a part in a West End show made me think it was really over.'

'Why?'

'Because that was like a statement of the direction in which her life was going, the direction in which she wanted it to go.'

'Sorry, you'll have to explain that to me.'

'Liddy and I met when we were at school. Then I did a Law degree, she did English, both at Nottingham Uni. We'd been together so long, it seemed logical to get married soon after we graduated.

'Liddy had always been keen on theatre, played lead roles in school productions, did lots of stuff at Nottingham. That didn't worry me. Law students had lots more lectures than people doing English, a much heavier workload, so it suited me fine that Liddy had an interest to keep her occupied when I was studying. Same thing when I was doing my Graduate Diploma and Legal Practice Course, right up until I was fully qualified.

'By then, Liddy was getting more involved in professional theatre – well, semi-professional, fringe stuff. And I was loyal. Theatre had never really been my thing, but I've lost count of the number of smelly upstairs rooms in pubs where I've been to watch Liddy in "experimental" – and, it has to be said, usually pretty dreadful – plays. She still had a day job round that time, teaching in a primary school, but she gradually cut down the hours she was putting in there to do more theatre. Still fine by me, because we'd always had this understanding that when I qualified, we'd start a family.

'So, when I did qualify, I assumed it would all be straightforward. We were late twenties, a lot of our contemporaries from school and uni were starting to have babies. It seemed logical that we should do the same.

'It was only when I raised the subject with Liddy that I realized how far our ambitions had drawn apart. She said her acting career was beginning to take off, and the last thing she wanted to do was to interrupt that progress by having a baby.

'I'd also told her that I was getting to the stage of my career when I was getting invitations to formal dinners and stuff, the kind of occasions which one should attend with one's wife. Liddy said she'd rather stick needles in her eyes than go to some "stuffed-shirt solicitors' event". I've done my best to keep the marriage going, but . . .'

Derek Litwood's narrative eventually trailed away to silence. Charles had only himself to blame. He was the one who'd asked for an explanation.

'So, when . . . I mean up until . . .' He tried to avoid mentioning the death, but couldn't. 'Up until Liddy died, what was the state of the marriage? Were you living together?'

'No. Nearly a year ago, we'd bought this lovely house in Muswell Hill, perfect for a family, and Liddy hardly stepped inside it.'

'Where was she living then?'

'With friends.' Derek shrugged. 'That's all she'd ever say. "With friends." I never knew where she was.'

'Didn't you know her friends? Couldn't you contact them?'

'I knew our mutual friends, obviously. You know, people in Muswell Hill. But her actor friends . . . Of course, I met some of them at First Nights and things, but I didn't *know* them. I didn't have any means of contacting them. So far as I was concerned, they were all interchangeable poseurs.'

Derek was unaware of the potential insult to the person he was sitting with. Charles was beginning to understand why Derek and Liddy's relationship had foundered. It was a syndrome he'd encountered many times before, where one member of a couple was 'in the business' and the other wasn't. One would arrive home, exhausted by a day's work, to find the other full of energy as they were about to go and give of themselves on stage. Then there were the different problems caused by touring and location filming. Charles didn't have to look a lot further than his own marriage. But he kept these thoughts to himself, just saying, 'Surely these days you can contact people through social media and stuff?'

'Yes, but at first, after Liddy walked out, I didn't want to contact her. Let her stew in her own juice for a while, I thought, and then she'll come back with her tail between her legs.' Derek was clearly unaware of mixed metaphors too. 'Then I did need to contact her. There were invitations addressed to both of us, local things and professional stuff, too. People at the office were starting to ask questions. When I did want to contact Liddy, she wouldn't answer the phone to me, though she did reply to texts about practical things. But I never knew where she was texting from. What she never seemed to realize,' he said bitterly, 'was how much a broken marriage could harm my career.'

A rather old-fashioned attitude, thought Charles. And then he realized that that was what defined Derek Litwood. He was deeply old-fashioned. All he wanted was a nice suburban house in Muswell Hill, with a wife who produced neat little children and scrubbed up well for solicitorial dinners. If that was a future Liddy Max had ever relished, working in the theatre had killed her appetite for it.

'So, had you talked about divorce?'

'No. She didn't think it was important, whether we actually ended the marriage officially or not. She said there was no point in getting divorced until one of us wanted to marry anyone else. I was quite pleased about that, because I genuinely thought that at some stage we would get back together.'

'Well, Liddy still wore a wedding ring, all the time we were rehearsing,' said Charles, hoping his words brought encouragement.

'Did she? Well, that doesn't mean anything with Liddy. Last time I saw her, she said she'd wear the ring in situations where there was a danger of some old lech coming on to her.'

'Oh,' said Charles, awkwardly remembering the thoughts that had gone through his head at *The Habit of Faith* read-through. He moved the conversation along. 'How long had you and Liddy been living apart?'

'Nearly a year now.' The abandoned husband looked gloomily into the residual foam of his cappuccino.

Charles made a connection. 'And am I right – the reason you came to the Duke of Kent's, you know, the afternoon of that Monday, was that you knew your wife would be there?'

Derek nodded. 'I'd seen publicity for the show in the paper, yes, and saw that Liddy was in it. I wanted to talk to her face to face, and finally I knew where I could find her.'

'So, had you been hanging round the theatre all that morning?'

'No, I'd only just arrived from the office. I asked the guy at the stage door if Liddy was in, and he said she'd just left for the coffee shop over the road.'

'I was in the coffee shop at the same time.'

'I know you were. I recognized you.'

'Oh?' Charles couldn't suppress the actor's kneejerk warm reaction to those words. He only just prevented himself from asking, 'What had you seen me in?'

Which was just as well, because Derek Litwood went on, 'I'd got the full cast list from the production company's website. Then I googled all the actors, and I saw a photo of you.'

Not quite as good as having been seen in a performance, but still quite cheering, just the fact that an image of Charles Paris was available online. He decided he must google himself as soon as he got back to his laptop. (Charles's mobile wasn't smart enough to access the internet – or, perhaps to put it more accurately, Charles wasn't smart enough to access the internet from his mobile.)

'Derek, can I ask about what was actually said between you, you know, that afternoon outside the coffee shop?'

'Oh, we went over a lot of old ground. I was hoping that she might have changed her mind a bit, but no. She was more determined than ever that her career was the only thing that mattered. She said she was just on the verge of a lot of exciting things happening in her life. She'd got a new agent, who wanted her to focus on work in the States. And she seemed to think that working with Justin Grover might help her to get a part in *Vandals and Visigoths*.'

'Was she specific about that? I mean, did she actually say she'd been offered a part?'

'No, she just thought working with him might lead to something. I should have realized when I first met her just how ambitious Liddy was. Success in acting was the only thing she cared about. Relationships, family, other people: none of them even registered with her.'

Charles made no comment. He'd met plenty of people in the theatre whom that description would fit, but he wouldn't have counted Liddy Max in their number. She had been devoted to her work, yes, but he had interpreted that as a desire to improve her skills, rather than to gain fame and money. Mind you, he hadn't really known her that well. Certainly not as well as her husband had. And Charles knew how distorted the views of partners in a failing marriage could be. He didn't really want to go there, because he felt sure Derek Litwood had an extensive further supply of recrimination to draw on.

So, rather tentatively, all he asked was: 'After you'd talked to Liddy, what did you do for the rest of the day?' If Derek had continued his surveillance of the stage door, there was no way he could have missed seeing Charles's arrival after the Alcoholics Anonymous meeting.

To his relief, the answer was that he had just gone back to work. And not returned to the Duke of Kent's that day.

'So, anyway, what was it you really wanted to ask me about, Derek?'

'Well, it's just . . . you were working with Liddy for the last few weeks. You probably know more about what she was up to than I do.'

'I wasn't working that closely with her. We didn't have many scenes together. And I didn't see her at all outside of work.'

'You were with her in the coffee shop.' It sounded like an accusation.

'That was the first time I'd ever gone out to eat with her.'

'Right.' The word was spoken grudgingly, as though Derek didn't really believe him. 'Listen, I said that for most of the last year Liddy was "with friends". Have you any idea who those "friends" were?'

With complete honesty, Charles said he hadn't.

'I suppose what I really want to know is whether it was "friends" or *a* "friend".'

'You mean – had she shacked up with another man?'

'That's exactly what I mean. I've been in touch with lots of our mutual friends, and none of them had any idea where she was living. She seemed to have gone to ground. I thought you might have – I don't know – seen her with some man at the theatre . . .?' There was a glint of growing paranoia in Derek Litwood's eyes.

'No,' said Charles. 'I didn't see her with anyone.'

'Did she talk about anyone?'

He decided not to reveal what Liddy had said about having a 'hot date'. He would keep that to himself for the time being. When he knew who the 'hot date' was, then he might share the information with Derek.

Maybe, his mind went on, encouraged by the memory leak he'd had in Liddy's dressing room, he might in time remember more of what he'd seen in the Duke of Kent's on the evening of her death.

Charles shrugged apologetically. 'I'm sorry, I'm not being much help.'

'No,' Derek agreed. Then, realizing that might sound rather rude, he went on, 'I'm just trying to get my head around what's happened.'

'I'm sorry. You must be in a very bad state.'

'More confused than anything, I think. I mean, if Liddy and I had still been together when she died, it'd be totally different. But in the last year, I've kind of recognized that the marriage is over . . . so, in a way, her death lets me off the hook.'

'How do you mean?' asked Charles, not sure he could believe what he was hearing.

'Well, I was in a marriage that wasn't working. My wife has died in tragic circumstances. That means I don't have to go through the ghastly process of a divorce. My path ahead is still a lot clearer than it was.'

'You mean, to meet someone, else? To remarry?'

'Yes,' Derek replied calmly. 'Someone who'll be content with her role as a wife and mother.'

'You'll be lucky to find one of those around these days,' was Charles's thought. But he didn't say it. He was still astonished by the calm, calculating way in which Derek Litwood spoke. He seemed to be suffering no pangs of bereavement. The loss of his wife had in fact proved very convenient for him. Charles wasn't surprised that Liddy had wanted out of marriage to such a cold-blooded creature.

Inevitably, with the thought of how convenient the death had been for her husband, came the suspicion that Derek might have engineered that death. But it seemed unlikely.

'What I did want to ask you, Charles,' the ungrieving widower went on, 'was whether you saw anything that evening – you know, the night she died.'

'I wasn't in the theatre, so I couldn't have seen anything.' There was no way he could go back on his lie now.

'No. As I said, the police won't tell me anything. Did any of the other members of the company see anything of what happened?'

'Why don't you ask them? Or have you already?'

'I haven't spoken to anyone else about Liddy. I will, obviously, if any of them have told you that they saw something strange.'

'Nobody has told me anything like that. I honestly don't think any other members of the company were in the theatre. We'd all suddenly got the bonus of a free evening, last one we were going to get – except Sundays – for three months. We'd be seeing quite enough of the Duke of Kent's over that period. Most of the cast wanted to enjoy their last night of freedom.'

'Except for Liddy.'

'Yes.'

'You've no idea why she might have stayed in the theatre?'

Charles felt even less inclined to mention the 'hot date'. 'No idea at all,' he said. 'I think we'll have to reconcile ourselves to the fact that this is one of those mysteries that can never be solved.'

But that didn't mean that Charles Paris wasn't determined to solve it.

It was as he walked up the stairs to his dressing room that Charles thought about the incongruity of the conversation he had just shared. Derek Litwood had singled him out from the rest of the company as a potential source of information. Why? Charles hadn't been particularly close to Liddy. When she socialized after rehearsal, it tended to be with Justin Grover and Grant Yeoell. Yet, from what Derek had said, he hadn't questioned either of them. Just Charles Paris.

It came to him suddenly. Not necessarily the truth, but a possible scenario. Derek Litwood had lied about not going back to the Duke of Kent's on the night his wife died. He had been keeping the place under surveillance, and seen Charles enter with his bottle of whisky soon after seven.

And the reason he'd wanted to question Charles was to find out whether Charles had witnessed what he, Derek, had done in the theatre that evening.

THIRTEEN

'Y ou going to have that drink tonight then?'
Charles was on his way out after the Tuesday show. He
was feeling virtuous about not having had a drink all day.
And even more virtuous about his intention to go straight back to
Hereford Road, where he no longer had a bottle of Bell's, and
complete the day alcohol-free.

On the other hand, it was Gideon doing the asking, and Charles
still felt there was more information he could get out of Gideon.

He said yes.

The stage doorman led him through the warren of streets off
Shaftesbury Avenue. It was an hour later. Gideon couldn't lock up
until everyone was out of the Duke of Kent's. Charles was aware of
the man's heavy breathing as they walked along. Just carrying that
enormous weight must be hard work. Gideon wasn't a healthy man.

He stopped at a rusty metal door round the back of another
theatre, and rapped on it with his knuckles.

'Like a speakeasy,' Charles murmured.

'It *is* a speakeasy,' said Gideon.

When the door was opened, the first thing that struck Charles
was the smell. Undertones of dampness that might have leaked from
a sewerage system but – dominating everything – alcohol. The
sourness of beer, the vinegar of old wine, the tang of spirits.

The venue had an air of impermanence. It was a cellar, possibly
some kind of disused storage facility. Solid brick steps led down
from the door. No decoration on the moist brick walls. Lighting
from stage lamps clipped to upright scaffolding, probably borrowed
or purloined from the local theatres. There was no bar as such, just
a table crowded with bottles and cans. The seating was a range of
run-down chairs, one or two painted in a way that suggested they
might once have been stage props.

The huddle of people inside turned with hostility towards the
newcomers, but relaxed when they saw the familiar bulk of Gideon.
He was clearly a regular.

'Let me get you a drink,' Charles offered.

'No worries. No money changes hands in here. Like a club it is, for the mutual benefit of its members.'

'So who pays for the booze?'

'A very generous theatre management. Now what would you like?'

'Scotch'd be good,' Charles replied instinctively.

'Any favourite?'

'Bell's.'

'Oh yes, I'd forgotten. Forgive me. Vodka and tonic man myself.' He poured generous measures for both of them. 'Water? Ice?'

'Bit of ice, thanks.'

Both took refreshing swallows. 'Sorry, Gideon, you said a generous theatre management sponsors this place?'

'Yes, they do.' He winked slyly. 'Mind you, I'm not sure they *know* that they do. Fact is, couple of the members here run the bars in two of our most prestigious West End theatres. It only takes a little bit of over-ordering, the odd bottle here, the odd bottle there and . . .' He raised his glass. 'A pure example of a theatre management really doing the best for their staff. God bless 'em.'

'What is this place, Gideon?'

'Used to be a store-room, used by a good few of the theatres, I believe, for props, lights, what-have-you. Then people forgot it was here and . . . well . . . as you see, we found a new use for it.'

'So how long has this set-up been going?'

'Yonks. I've been coming since I started working at the Duke of Kent's. And that's over five years. Supplies a need, this place. Everyone here works in the theatre, you see. Very few actors or directors, some writers come along. That Seamus Milligan – you know, miserable sod who wrote *Habit* – he's in here sometimes. But it's not basically for the *artistic* lot.' He loaded the word with a lot of pretension. 'We're all techies and ancillary. But we work strange hours. Often don't get out of the theatre until after the pubs have closed. And, all right, there are plenty of clubs in the West End where you can drink the night away, but we can't afford their prices. Besides, we don't want to go somewhere you have to smarten up for. Just hang out with our mates, that's what we want to do. So, if you know about this place, you can get a drink here right through the night.'

'Does it actually have opening hours?'

Gideon snorted away the suggestion. 'Not officially. There are a few people who've got keys.' The arch way this was said suggested he might be one of them. 'Someone usually opens up tennish, or a bit earlier, now you've got so many ninety-minute shows that run through without an interval. And, generally, someone locks up round six in the morning.'

'And you've never had any trouble with the police? About licensing or—?'

'Never happens. They don't mess with us, we don't mess with them.'

'Well, we do sometimes mess with them.' The new voice came from a small man in grubby denims. His personal odour was strong enough to assert itself over the predominant smells of the cellar. His eyes had the glaze of the permanently drunk.

'Hi, Baz,' said Gideon. 'Might have known you'd turn up like a bad penny. Baz, this is Charles Paris. He's in the show we got in the Duke of Kent's.'

'Play with all those bloody monks maundering on, and Justin Grover poncing around in a cassock?'

'That's the one, right.' Charles thought it was a pretty fair description. 'You sound like you've seen it.'

Both men roared with laughter, as Gideon explained, 'Point of honour, Charles. Stage doormen never go and see the shows.'

'So, are you a stage doorman too, Baz?'

'Well, I was, like.' The small man looked embarrassed. 'Didn't work out.'

'Touch of the old "Drunk in Charge of a Theatre", wasn't it?' The flesh around Gideon's neck wobbled as he roared with laughter.

'Yeah, something like that.' It was clear from Baz's expression that he wished his friend hadn't brought the matter up. But Charles wondered whether Baz's example was one of the reasons why Gideon had been so paranoid about the threat posed to his own job by his drinking habit.

'Actually,' the small man went on, 'I've been wanting to see you, Gid, because I had a dead funny—'

'Yeah, we can talk about that later,' said the stage doorman rather grandly, as he swept off to greet another friend. 'Hello, Morry . . .'

The look with which Baz followed Gideon's departure was so achingly forlorn that Charles realized how much the man felt for his friend. Even Gideon could inspire love. And perhaps toy with the affections of someone who loved him.

Disconsolately, Baz picked up a vodka bottle from the table and took a long pull.

'So, are you working now?' asked Charles.

Baz shook his head. 'No. Nobody will employ me.' Charles didn't have to ask why. 'Still spend my time around the West End. Got a lot of mates in the business who help me out. And I can always find somewhere to kip down here.'

Also, always find plenty of free booze down here too, thought Charles. His glass was empty. The instinct to top it up from the Scotch bottle was very strong. But he decided to resist it.

'And you've known Gideon for a long time?'

'Since I first started working in the West End. Don't know how long ago that is. It's good to have mates.'

'Certainly is.' Charles watched as Baz took another swig from the vodka bottle.

'Yeah,' Baz agreed. 'Mates do each other favours. Gid's always doing favours for people, like people who're working in the Duke of Kent's. Always some little job needs doing there. And Gid's always ready to oblige. Mind you, those jobs he does for money, nice cash in hand. Mates help each other out for free. That's what mates are for.'

Charles couldn't argue with the sentiment, but he saw that it opened out a possible line of enquiry. 'So, have you helped Gideon out sometimes?'

'Yes, sure. And he's helped me, and all.'

'Oh? How's he helped you?'

'He sometimes brings me food and stuff. Lets me kip on his floor sometimes.' This was said with wistfulness.

'And how have you helped him?'

'Oh.' A slyness came into the glazed eyes. 'I've helped him in lots of ways. Recently I helped him from getting into trouble.'

'Trouble from his employers? From the Duke of Kent's?'

'Maybe them. Maybe trouble from the police,' he added proudly.

'What do you mean?'

'There was a problem at the Duke of Kent's . . . I can't remember when . . . a few weeks ago?'

'What kind of problem?'

'Somebody died there.' Baz seemed to have forgotten Charles's

connection with the theatre. He spoke as if to someone unfamiliar
with the news of Liddy's death.

'But what's that got to do with Gideon?' asked Charles.

'Well, this day, whenever it was, there was no rehearsal for
some reason, and Gideon had nothing to do, so I suggested, like,
he come out drinking with me. But he was worried about leaving
the stage door unmanned, you know, if someone from the management found he wasn't there. 'Cause they've got those CCTV
cameras all round the back of the theatre. So I said I'd sort it.'
There was no doubting the pride with which this assertion was
made.

'What did you do, Baz?'

'It's a little trick I've got – get asked to do it quite a lot, actually.
There's plenty of people round the West End who sometimes do
things they don't want to have recorded on the old CCTV. If I'm
nippy, I can sort it out for them, never get caught. And I make a bit
of spending money, or they buy me a drink, or . . . you know . . .'

'I'm sorry, what are you saying, that you manage to switch off
CCTV cameras?'

'Not switch them off, blank them out.'

'I'm still not with you.'

'I'll show you.' Baz led him across to a corner of the room
that the spotlights hardly reached. Against the wall were a couple
of rusty leather boxes about the size of old cabin trunks. On
top of them was an assortment of cables, props and other theatrical impedimenta, perhaps dating from the time when the cellar
had been used as a store-room.

'This is my kit,' said Baz proudly, picking up a thin cylinder
about eighteen inches long with a series of metal rings sticking out
from it.

'What on earth's that?'

'Collapsible fishing rod.' He pulled at it to show how the staff
extended. 'Use that, bit of sponge on the end, dip it in some dark
paint, and Bob's your uncle! Covers over the lens of a CCTV camera
in no time.'

'Isn't it risky? I mean, someone might see you doing it.'

'I choose my moments. Haven't got caught yet. Anyway, everything we do in life is risky.' There was a bravado in Baz's manner.
He seemed to be saying: there may be many things I can't do, but
this is one that I can, and I do it very well.

'But,' asked Charles, 'why did you disable the CCTV camera that particular day? Did Gideon ask you to do it?'

'No, but I knew he had time off, and I wanted him to come drinking with me, but he said he couldn't leave the theatre, because of the CCTV camera, so I . . .' Baz glowed with pride. 'I sorted it out for him.'

'And he then did come drinking with you? Here?'

'Yes. He was afraid, if he went to any of the pubs, someone from the theatre management might see him.'

'What, so he was with you here all that afternoon and evening? Until he went back to lock up the theatre just before twelve?'

Baz looked uncertain. 'It's a long time ago. I can't remember exactly.' His eyes shifted across the room. He didn't like what he saw. Charles followed his look. Gideon was still deep in conversation with the 'Morry' whom he'd joined earlier.

'Baz, it's important. Did Gideon leave here for the theatre just before midnight, or did he go earlier?'

'I can't remember.'

'Please. Try to focus on that day.'

Baz's glazed eyes didn't look as if they could focus on anything. As if in a trance, he moved back to the table with the drinks, picked up the vodka bottle and necked about a quarter of it. He turned back to Charles. 'Yes, Gid went back to the theatre earlier. Came back here soon after.'

'And then stayed till near midnight?'

'No, he wasn't here long. Just dumped some stuff and left. I remember, because I wanted him to stay. Wanted him to stay with me. But he went. He can be very cruel sometimes, Gid.' Baz looked across to where the stage doorman had one of his pudgy arms around Morry's waist. 'Like he's being now.'

'You said he dumped some stuff, Baz. What kind of stuff?'

'I don't know.' He seemed to be losing interest in their conversation; he was becoming consumed with jealousy about his friend's behaviour.

'Where did he put the stuff?'

'Over there.' A vague gesture towards the metal boxes in the corner. Then Baz took another substantial swig from the vodka bottle and, holding it like a baseball bat, moved forward, full of anger. 'What the hell do you think you're playing at, Gid?'

The raised voices and the imminent threat of violence roused the other drinkers in the cellar. They didn't want any scenes in their private club. Nothing that might draw unwanted attention to them. They moved forward to separate and pacify the combatants. Within a few moments, all three men – Baz, Gideon and Morry – had been persuaded to leave.

Charles hoped he wouldn't be turned out as well, now that he was without his escort, but nobody seemed that interested in him. He drifted across towards the metal boxes.

Apart from Baz's equipment, there was an incredible jumble of stuff piled on top of them. Much of it was covered with the dust of years, but shinier surfaces told of more recent arrivals.

It was the colour that drew his attention. Deep apricot. Like the interior of Liddy Max's dressing room. It had been painted over the black gaffer tape.

Charles picked up the object, feeling the stickiness of the tape, which told him it hadn't been there long. He moved into the light. What was revealed, with the apricot-painted gaffer tape attached, was a black metal object about the shape and the size of an eyeball.

Charles Paris had never seen one before, but he felt pretty certain he knew what it was.

FOURTEEN

On the Wednesday, he got in earlier than he needed to have done for the matinee. Before the rest of the cast.

Gideon wasn't in his cubby-hole. This was unusual. Charles wondered if the stage doorman's drinking (and who knew what else) session with Morry the night before had taken its toll.

Anyway, Gideon's absence was good news for Charles. He nipped into the cubby-hole and removed two keys from the board of hooks where they were kept.

On the first landing, he didn't go up the next flight to his own dressing room. Instead he turned towards the one that was now Imogen Whittaker's, but had belonged to Liddy Max.

When he opened the door, he knew exactly what he had to do. He took out of his pocket the object he had found in the Techie's Drinking Club and moved towards the apricot-painted pipes.

Yes, as he had speculated and hoped, the edges of the ripped and overpainted gaffer tape fitted exactly with the shreds which remained. The object had once been fixed to those pipes.

But he hardly had time to feel a glow of satisfaction before a voice behind him said, 'What the hell do you think you're doing, Charles?'

It was Kell. He moved guiltily back towards the door. 'Since when has this been your dressing room?' she demanded.

'I just took the key. Gideon wasn't in his cubby-hole.'

'That's hardly the point. This is still Imogen's dressing room. I hadn't got you down, Charles, as the kind of man who gets off on rooting through women's possessions.'

'And I am certainly not that kind of man.'

'Then what the hell are you doing here?'

He held out the small plastic object in his hand. 'I have reason to believe that, until quite recently, this was fixed up in here.' He held it up against the pipes, to show where it had been torn away.

'And have you just ripped it off?'

'No. Gideon did.'

'How do you know?'

'That'll take a bit of explaining. I went with him—'

'Yes, I'm sure it will,' Kell cut in. 'When did he remove it?'

'If what I'm thinking's right, he did it after he'd found Liddy's body.'

'Ah. You know what it is, don't you, Charles?'

'I'm assuming it's some kind of spy camera.'

Kell nodded. 'Yes, the bloody things are getting so miniaturized now.'

'Would there be a way of finding out what it was recording?'

'I think we could probably guess, but, yes, I've got leads and things at home with which I could access the footage.' Of course. Charles had forgotten about Kell's computer science degree. 'I'll check it out when I get home tonight. That is, if you're prepared to let me take it . . .'

She held out her hand. It never occurring to him not to trust her, Charles handed the tiny camera across. 'You reckon we're dealing with a Peeping Tom?'

'That would certainly be one explanation.'

'Gideon?'

'If what you say is correct, and he did remove the camera after Liddy's death, then the finger would seem to point at him, yes.'

'Have you had any message from him, about when he's going to be in?'

'Nothing. I've been on to the theatre management. They're sending someone over as a stand-in.'

'Do you reckon he's done a runner?'

'It certainly looks that way,' said Kell.

'Now, for those of you who haven't been here before . . . Charles . . . I should start with a quick word about confidentiality. Whatever is said in Gower House stays in Gower House. Are you all clear about that?' The disparate group in the room mumbled assent. 'These meetings only work if you all feel absolutely confident that you can talk freely, and that no one's going to shop you to employers, family members or the cops? OK?'

Another mumbled agreement. The walls of this room were unadorned, just painted white. The floorboards were stripped and varnished. Tall windows opened out on to a well-maintained garden, whose end fence was the boundary of the garden of an equally grand mansion in a mirror-image row of grand mansions on the parallel street. Charles wondered whether the other residents of this genteel, well-heeled North London location knew what went on in Gower House.

The answer was probably yes. There were few secrets in suburbia. It was quite possible that, when the locals found out what use the premises were going to be put to, they had protested to the local authorities. They hadn't invested their millions in Finchley properties to have their privacy invaded by swarms of alcoholics and drug addicts. They didn't want their front gardens peed on. They didn't want their streets littered with empty bottles and used syringes. They didn't want their houses burgled by crazed losers desperate for their next fix.

But Charles was conjecturing, when he knew he should be concentrating on the matter in hand. He had arrived in good time at a quarter to twelve on the Thursday for his first 'Growing Out' meeting, and he had felt disproportionately nervous. It was like being about to go on stage for the first night of an iffy new play, of whose lines he had only a very precarious grasp.

He had managed to get through the two shows on the Wednesday and make it back to Hereford Road without having a drink. When he woke on the Thursday, he would have observed how much better he felt than he did most mornings, had not the anxiety about his forthcoming session at Gower House blanked out all other emotions.

He had encountered the same guarded friendliness in the waiting room, and again refused offers of a hot drink. A coffee might have helped to ease his nerves but, even though he hadn't drunk the night before, he still didn't feel sure he could hold a mug without spilling it.

The conversation about him was predictable male banter, a lot of 'How're you doing?' and mild discussion of the previous night's football. He didn't feel confident enough to join in, just made sure he was smiling when anyone looked at him. Somebody remembered that they needed to switch off their mobile phones before the meeting started. Charles followed suit.

He'd kind of supposed that Erica would be leading the 'Growing Out' session, but they were asked to go upstairs by a man who identified himself as 'Ricky'. Probably fifteen years younger than Charles, he wore jeans, Converse sneakers and a T-shirt featuring

some band Charles had never heard of. It was clear that the other
participants all knew Ricky well.

'Have you all signed in?' he asked. There was a clipboard with
a ruled sheet on it, and two columns, one to enter your name and
the other to put in a tick or cross, according to whether you intended
to be at the next week's session. Charles put in a dutiful tick, but
was by no means certain that he would attend more than once. His
attitude remained one of detached scepticism. He was there because
he looked forward to getting a brownie point from Frances when
he told her, but he wasn't convinced that this regime – or any kind
of regime – was for him. It wasn't as though he had a serious
problem. He was attending TAUT rather in the way he might have
attended a Speeding Awareness Course, to avoid getting more penalty
points from Frances.

As the session progressed, and he heard more about the dire
situations which had brought the other participants to Gower House,
the more the conviction grew that his problem was not a very serious
one.

The meeting started with a check-in. Each person present would
say their first name, then select a number between one and ten to
define their current state of mind or mood, and assess how the past
week had been for them. Then they had to say what they thought
they could bring to the session, and what they hoped to get out of it.

Charles, as the newest arrival in the group, waited till all the
others had checked in. He assessed his state of mind as 'five', but
didn't answer the question about his last week. He reckoned that
one was more for the regulars, who could make comparisons with
previous statements. He had heard them in their individual check-
ins, marking themselves for their days of total abstinence, their
progress in cutting down or, in some cases, serious backsliding.
These revelations were greeted by commendation or sympathy from
the other participants, but not with the manic glad-handing that
Charles had found so deterrent at the Alcoholics Anonymous
meeting.

Continuing to follow the unwritten questionnaire, Charles
confessed that he wasn't sure what he could bring to the meeting,
and, as to what he wanted to get out of it, produced some woolly
phrases about 'hoping to get a better understanding of his behaviour'.
Nobody questioned what he had said, so he reckoned he'd come
through the first test all right.

Ricky then wrote a single word in green felt pen on the flipchart. It was 'TRIGGERS'. And he said he wanted the group to talk about what triggered their recourse – though he didn't use the word 'recourse' – to drink or drugs. (Charles noticed that the session addressed both addictions, and some of the participants clearly had problems with both.)

As the group discussed their 'triggers', certain patterns emerged. The predominant reason was a reaction to stress. Whether it was an overly demanding job, a failing relationship, money worries or a thousand other aggravations, the oblivion offered by drink or drugs was instantly appealing. Ricky suggested that this arose from 'an unwillingness to face reality', and no one argued against that. But the way he said the words was not critical.

Charles also observed that, in almost all cases, the group members pointed back to some major 'trigger', some traumatic event that had started their abuse. A couple cited divorce, one man had lost his job, a marathon fanatic had sustained a knee injury that had put an end to his running career, and a woman cited the cot death of her first child.

When Charles asked himself if there was some similar shock in his own life that had pushed him towards the drink, he couldn't think of one. He'd just always liked the stuff.

But, faced with a direct question from Ricky about his 'triggers', the situations in which he would find himself reaching for the bottle, Charles replied, 'Well, it often happens after a period of intense concentration. You know, you've been doing some work and that's been your complete focus, and then you finish it, and having a drink makes you relax quicker. It helps the unwinding process.'

What he was referring to, of course, was the state of heightened adrenaline experienced at the end of a performance, but for some reason he didn't want to tell the rest of the group that he was an actor. He knew that some people felt a lot of prejudice against his profession.

'So, if that's the trigger,' Ricky responded gently, 'might there be a way of not putting yourself in that situation?'

'How do you mean? Not getting pumped up about the . . . the piece of work that I've been doing?' It was going to be difficult to keep the details of that work secret for any length of time. 'I'm afraid it just wouldn't be possible.'

'No, I'm not saying you shouldn't put so much energy into your

work. I'm saying that you could maybe avoid the situation you find
yourself in when you've finished, which means you're going to have
a drink straight away.'

'Not going straight down the pub when you've clocked off,'
suggested the one who'd lost his job.

'Yes,' Ricky agreed. 'Something like that. Make sure, when you've
finished your work, you're not in a place where there's any alcohol
available.'

'Ye-es,' said Charles, unconvinced. He knew himself too well. If
a show went down after the pubs were closed, he'd always make sure
he'd got a bottle of Bell's in his dressing room. And then he came
up with the lame excuse that: 'There tend to be other people involved,
people you've been working with and, you know, not to go round
the pub with them . . . well, it can look a bit antisocial.'

'It is possible,' suggested one of the divorcees, 'to go round the
pub and not have an alcoholic drink.'

This concept was totally alien to Charles. As he struggled to
regain his composure, the other divorcee said, 'And doing that can
make you feel really good – you know, you've faced the temptation
and you've resisted it.'

This sounded, for Charles's taste, far too like Tod Singer's
comments in the pub after *The Habit of Faith* read-through. He
wondered how long he was going to be able to survive the TAUT
regime.

He was still wondering, as he left Gower House and started off
towards the tube. Though the easy camaraderie had been maintained
while they were inside the building, once outside, the participants
all acted as if they had never seen each other before. Though some
of them had the same destination, there was no attempt to walk
together or chat to anyone. Charles could understand how there might
be a reluctance to recognize other addicts in a public situation.

He was also struck by how many of the group lit up cigarettes
the moment they got outside. Clearly, dealing with one addiction
at a time.

Charles assessed the hour he had just spent. Though some of the
things said had been statements of the bleeding obvious, there were
other comments which had made an impression on him. He had
also respected the openness and honesty with which the group
members had contributed to the discussion. He had said virtually

nothing, except when asked direct questions, but he could see how he might be emboldened to offer more of his own opinions on another occasion.

If, of course, there was another occasion. He hadn't yet made up his mind about that. Though he had found the atmosphere considerably less cloying than the religiosity of Alcoholics Anonymous, Charles was still not certain it was for him. The one thing about the set-up that did appeal was the thought of the check-in, of appearing the following week to announce he'd had a couple of days off the booze. There was a competitive element in that which appealed to him.

He also couldn't repress a slight smugness. Yes, he drank too much, but the consequences of his drinking had not been as devastating as those described by some of the other participants. He hadn't had his house repossessed, he hadn't had his children taken into care, he hadn't been hospitalized or imprisoned as a result of his drinking. He wasn't as bad as they were.

But, even as he had the thought, he knew it was a dangerous one.

Anyway, there was a whole week ahead in which to decide whether he ever went back to Gower House. In the meantime, he should, as soon as possible, tell Frances that he'd been there that morning. Hopefully, a first step in rehabilitating himself in her eyes. He switched his mobile back on.

It was a school day, so he didn't call her. Texting was probably the answer, just to make her aware of his considerable achievement. Then, he could phone her after she'd got back from school, just before the evening's performance of *The Habit of Faith* started.

But, as his mobile came back to life, a tone informed him that there was a text waiting.

'Charles, I've accessed the footage on the spy camera. Very interesting. If you come to the theatre round five this evening, I'll have time to show you. Kx.'

So, he'd got an 'x' that time.

FIFTEEN

'You were right, Charles,' said Kell grimly.

They were in her office, one of the basement dressing rooms that had been allocated to the stage management. Dark flowerings of damp were coming through the paint on the walls. There were no personal touches in the room beyond her zip-up waterproof coat hanging on the back of the door. There was a couch, piled up with boxes of copy paper and other stationery, which didn't give the impression that she got much chance to lie on it and relax. In fact, there was nothing to suggest she spent much time there. The only other furniture was a wooden chair and a table on which sat a laptop and a printer.

She pointed at the screen, then touched something on the metal eyeball Charles had found. It was now connected by a lead to her computer. She moved the eyeball around, and on the screen appeared images of the parts of the room it pointed at.

'So, it is a camera?'

'Spy camera, yes,' Kell confirmed.

'And does it just show live action?' he asked, though he knew what the answer would be.

'No. It records too,' replied Kell wearily.

'But someone could still watch a live relay?'

'Oh yes.'

'On what?'

She shrugged. 'Virtually anything these days. Desktop, laptop, tablet, smartphone.'

'And is there any way of telling whose machine it's been watched on?'

'Might be if you could check their machine. But since you don't know whose machine it is, that might be a bit tricky.'

Charles recognized that he had been optimistic. 'So, what have you got?' he asked.

'Only a couple of bits.'

'Oh?'

'Think about it, Charles. That Monday was the first time we'd been in the theatre. The dressing room had presumably been locked up since the last show finished the week before. The dressing rooms weren't allocated till lunchtime. So, assuming the camera was set up to spy on Liddy, it wouldn't have started recording until she first entered the room that day.'

'What, is it switched on remotely?'

'Charles, these things are motion-detecting. They switch themselves on when they sense movement in the room. I'll show you.' Kell pressed a few buttons on her laptop. 'I downloaded this.'

Given the size of the camera, the picture quality was surprisingly good. The recording started just as Liddy switched the light on and closed the door after entering her dressing room. She was dressed in what she'd worn for rehearsal on that Monday morning. She looked around the room that she thought was going to be hers for the next three months. She put her bag and the door key down on the ledge in front of the mirror – their rattle was very clear on the recording – then leant forward to check her make-up. Satisfied that it would pass muster, she moved out of shot. There was the sound of a door opening, presumably to the bathroom. Charles was very grateful the camera couldn't follow her in there. There was already something very uncomfortable about seeing Liddy so very alive on the day of her death, without any further assault on her dignity.

The screen went blank for a very short moment, then showed Liddy coming back into shot, doing up the belt of her jeans. Another quick check in the mirror prompted her to take a brush out of her bag and tidy her hair. Then she picked up her belongings and, having switched the light off, left the room. The camera seemed to wait for the sound of her door being locked from the outside, before switching itself off.

Kell paused the playback.

'So that,' said Charles, 'would be when she came downstairs to the Green Room and we all went off for lunch at the coffee shop?'

'Has to be. Unfortunately, a little gadget like this isn't sophisticated enough to have a time code.' She looked at Charles, her expression still grim. 'Do you feel up to watching the next bit?'

He nodded, and Kell pressed the button. She fast-forwarded through some footage of Liddy Max entering her dressing room, switching on the light, disappearing out of shot and reappearing dressed in a monk's habit. At that point, Kell readjusted the replay to normal speed.

There was a knock on the door. Liddy Max opened it, to admit a figure in a monk's habit, with the cowl over his head. The angle at which he entered and shielded his face suggested that he knew where the camera was.

With the minimum of preparation, and no conversation, the hooded man embraced the girl. She seemed ready for him, clutching at him. He lifted her to sit on the ledge in front of her make-up mirror. She opened her legs to wrap around him and the couple made urgent love.

'Are you going to tell the police about this?' asked Charles.

'Why would I do that?' asked Kell. There was a silence. Then she asked, 'Are you?'

'Why would I do that?' asked Charles.

Kell had things to do, and it was a very thoughtful Charles Paris who climbed up the stairs to his dressing room. He still had more than an hour before the 'half' (that magic cut-off point, thirty-five minutes before curtain-up, when all the company must have checked in before a performance. Arriving at the theatre after the 'half' was a major crime in the canon of thespian law.)

He sat in front of his mirror, feeling shock and a variety of attendant emotions. His first reaction was to reach into his bag for the habitual half-bottle of Bell's that lived there. But he realized he hadn't got one. The impact of his 'Growing Out' meeting at Gower House that morning had stopped him from buying a replacement for the last empty.

Oh well, he'd just have to think without alcoholic stimulus.

The footage he had just seen prompted two major questions. Who was Liddy's lover? And who had set up the camera to spy on her in her dressing room?

The first was the more difficult to answer. The cowl worn by the man making love to Liddy made him hard to identify with any certainty. As Charles had observed earlier, all the male actors in *The Habit of Faith* were more or less the same height. And the way the lover did not speak and moved around the room, keeping his back to the camera, suggested that he knew it was there.

Of course, the man need not have been a member of the company. Liddy had spoken of having a 'hot date', but that could easily have been someone who had nothing to do with the theatre. It could even have been her husband. From what he'd said, a reconciliation with

Derek had sounded unlikely, but who could say what went on inside a marriage? And the ease with which the pair had coupled suggested some level of familiarity. Maybe they'd got to the point in their relationship where they could only make love when dressed as monks?

But no, Charles could not produce certain identification of the man involved without further research.

The question about who had planted the camera in Liddy's dressing room – and for whose gratification it had been planted there – was easier to answer. In fact, there was only one suspect.

While Charles Paris, in keeping with contemporary right-on thinking, tried not to be ageist, sexist or a proliferating number of other 'ists', he could not help recognizing that Gideon was not high up in the animal magnetism stakes. Though the stage doorman seemed able to inspire devotion in Baz (and possibly Morry), his success in the traditional dating stakes might well not have been high. For someone like Gideon to get his kicks in less conventional ways, like voyeurism, did not seem an unlikely scenario.

Also, Gideon knew the Duke of Kent's Theatre intimately. He had probably – a fact Charles could check with Kell – been informed of the allocation of dressing rooms for *The Habit of Faith* before any of the company. So he would have known which one would be occupied by the only female member of the cast, Liddy Max. With all the keys available on the board in his cubby-hole, Gideon would have been uniquely placed to enter that dressing room and plant his spy camera.

And, if that were not enough evidence to convict the stage doorman as a Peeping Tom, Charles knew for a fact that it was Gideon who had ripped out the camera and dumped it in the Techie's Drinking Club.

Now, as if to confirm his guilt to anyone who still had any doubts about it, Gideon had done a runner.

No, identifying the suspect had not presented Charles with too much of a problem. Actually finding that suspect might offer more of a challenge.

He checked his watch. Still nearly an hour before the 'half'. Well, it was worth trying.

Working on hunches sometimes worked and sometimes didn't. When it did, Charles felt he was on an incredible high. On the right track, his judgement had been vindicated, and nothing could stand between him and the result he was hoping for.

That's what he felt when, at quarter past six that evening, he found the door to the 'Techie's Drinking Club' unlocked.

He didn't have a torch with him, and he didn't need it. None of the spotlights was on, but a small lamp on the drinks table was.

Gideon lay flat on his back, his vast stomach rising from the floor like some geographical feature. Three empty vodka bottles stood upright by his side.

As Charles drew closer, he could smell the acrid vomit, on which the stage doorman had choked away his life.

SIXTEEN

'I've had three days in the last week without a drink.'

'Charles, you didn't give a figure for your current mood. Out of ten?'

'Oh, I suppose . . . two.'

'You shouldn't be feeling so low if you've done three days without a drink. You should be feeling proud of yourself.'

'No, it's nothing to do with the booze. It's . . . other, personal things.'

Ricky was far too tactful to ask for anything more.

Charles was surprised to find himself at the 'Growing Out' session for a second time. In the course of the week, he had been through a variety of attitudes to the TAUT set-up. After the shock of finding Gideon's body, his emotions had been even more volatile.

But what had swayed it for him, what had taken him back to Gower House, was the desire to report back to his fellow attendees the three days he had coped without a drink. It was a strange kind of brownie pointage he was after, an aspiration that he couldn't really explain, but that felt important to him.

He had told no one, not even Kell, about what he had found in the Techie's Drinking Club. Unwilling to invite further encounters with the police, he reasoned that Gideon's body would be found soon enough by somebody else. And so it proved. On the Thursday morning, Kell had sent out a text to all the company, announcing the stage doorman's death. She provided no details of how it had happened, but said the theatre management would be sending appropriate condolences to his family.

Charles wondered who that family was. He realized that he knew very little about Gideon, apart from the fact that he had problems with drinking and voyeurism. Maybe somewhere there would be a worshipping mother unhinged by grief at her bereavement? Maybe Baz would be equally affected? Possibly even Morry?

The thought of Baz suggested to Charles that he should try to track him down. Baz was Gideon's drinking companion. He might know more about the circumstances of his friend's death. He might even have been with him for that final session with the vodka . . .? But Charles wouldn't know where to start trying to find someone who lived on the streets.

He wondered whether the police knew of Gideon's connection with Baz. Since his own interview with them, he had wondered a lot about what the police knew, how their investigation into Liddy Max's death was going. Presumably, they hadn't already tied up the case with a neat bow, concluding it was an unexplained accident? Or maybe they had? What had the poor girl's post mortem revealed? As Charles now knew, her body would have shown signs of recent sexual activity. Though ignorant of such forensic matters, he reckoned that Liddy's unknown lover, even if he had worn a condom, would have left some physical record of their encounter.

And yet he hadn't heard of any of *The Habit of Faith* company being asked to provide DNA samples. Not for the first time, Charles Paris felt frustrated by the inscrutability of official enquiries. Outside the realms of Golden Age detective stories, the police had never shown much enthusiasm for sharing their findings with amateurs.

Still, presumably at some point there would be an inquest into Liddy Max's death. And Gideon's, come to that. Maybe more information would emerge then.

The word written that day on the flipchart in Gower House was 'Change', and the participants were discussing the difficulties of making changes that might help them control their addiction. Charles was struck by the choice of words that Ricky used. He could have said 'conquer' addiction, but he deliberately selected 'control'. The TAUT method did not offer quick fixes. It was not proscriptive in the way of Alcoholics Anonymous. Total abstinence might be the ultimate goal of its therapy, but it recognized that there were other achievable advances on the way to that state.

He was once again struck by the honesty of the people sitting in the circle with him. Though addicts are notoriously mendacious about their habits, in that room there seemed to be no point in lying. They respected the confidentiality that they had agreed to, and benefited from the opportunity to talk. Charles recognized that the participants came from a wide range of backgrounds. Only a few shared with him the advantage of a university education. One couldn't even read. But all were prepared to communicate. And some of their stories – like that of the scaffolder who couldn't go up a ladder first thing in the morning without half a bottle of vodka inside him – Charles found amazing.

But within the last week, there had been a subtle change in his attitude. At the first session, he had stood outside the group, congratulating himself on the fact that his problems were not as severe as theirs. Now there was a sliver of an idea in his brain that his addiction might be part of the same narrative.

As the session went on, Charles once again found himself wondering what 'TAUT' stood for. He must remember to ask Ricky at the end.

But when the hour and a half was up, he forgot the question, because the facilitator wanted a word about something else. Charles's worries that he might have said something inappropriate during the meeting were quickly allayed. Ricky was just wondering whether he might like to try attending the 'Weekend Group' at four the following day. 'It's less structured, just you and the other participants chatting amongst yourselves, really, but you're clearly articulate, and might find it useful.'

To his surprise, Charles found himself agreeing to the suggestion.

And forgetting to ask what 'TAUT' stood for.

Weeks passed, without a lot of progress on the investigation front. *The Habit of Faith* cast seemed to forget that Liddy Max had ever been part of the company. Imogen Whittaker grew into the role of The Girl and started getting a lot of attention, being lined up for fashion shoots and having her dating history chronicled in gossip columns. The *A Star is Born* understudy-takes-over scenario seemed to be working out very well. But Charles couldn't for the life of him work out any way of implicating her in the death of Liddy Max.

The excitement about Imogen's potential grew when it was heard among the cast that Justin Grover had invited one of the American producers of *Vandals and Visigoths* to see *The Habit of Faith*. This could have been merely a professional courtesy, but the rumour grew that his visit was, on Justin's recommendation, to check out the potential of Imogen Whittaker as a new character in the expanding movie franchise. The suggestion led to a lot of backstage jealousy – and a lot of overacting at the relevant performance as other actors tried to make their impression on the producer.

The departure of Gideon from the scene caused even less of a ripple. Though a stage doorman is part of the fabric of a theatre, he is distinct from the play's company, and his replacement, a very camp ex-actor called Wallace, slipped easily into the vacant role.

So, Charles Paris continued in his unrewarding role as Brother Benedict, The Monk Who Just Listened To All Of The Other Monks Who Maundered On In Long Speeches About Their Own Internal Conflicts. Oh well, he was getting paid West End money.

The promised late-night drinking sessions with Kell didn't materialize.

But Sunday lunch with Frances – and without alcohol – became something of a fixture.

It was five weeks into the run when, on the ribbon-trellised board by Wallace's cubby-hole, appeared a flurry of pink envelopes addressed by hand to all company members, acting and backstage. They contained invitations from Justin Grover to after-show drinks to celebrate his birthday. The venue was the room in the Duke of Kent's where they'd been entertained after the Press Night, and the date was a Thursday.

This presented Charles Paris with an unaccustomed dilemma. During the previous weeks, because Thursday was the evening between his 'Growing Out' and his 'Weekend Group' meetings at Gower House, he had got into the habit of making it one of his non-drinking days. Was it possible that he might go to a backstage party and not drink? He had heard of leopards changing their spots, but that would be a total tiger-skin transplant.

Charles only had a brief conversation with Kell about Gideon's death. She told him the police – the same two, Tricker and Bowles – had interviewed her again. 'Just logistics, really. When I'd last seen him in the theatre, that kind of thing.'

'Anything specific about how he'd died?'

'Nothing that hasn't already been round the company.'

'So, what did they ask you, specifically?'

'The only questions that weren't to do with timings were about his personality. Whether I'd ever seen him being violent towards anyone in the company? Which, of course, I hadn't.'

'Do you think they were suspicious that he might have attacked Liddy?'

Kell shrugged. 'That's a possible interpretation, but they certainly didn't suggest that. The impression they gave was that they were just tying up the loose ends, you know, finishing the paperwork.'

'Did they say any more about Liddy?'

She shook her head. 'They didn't mention her. I asked them if they thought the two deaths were connected, and they went all official on me. "Investigations are still proceeding", you know, all that stuff. But again I got the impression they were just wrapping things up.'

'So, going on from their question about Gideon possibly being violent,' he persisted, 'they might have concluded that he pushed Liddy down the stairs?'

'They might, Charles, they might not. You might think that. I might think that. As is customary with members of the constabulary, Tricker and Bowles volunteered the minimum of information about their mental processes.'

And that was as near as Charles Paris got to the official conclusions about the deaths connected with the Duke of Kent's Theatre.

Justin Grover was in expansive mood at his birthday party. 'I haven't invited any of the producers along,' he announced, 'because I want this to be a fun occasion.'

Charles recognized the tactic. All actors have an ambivalent attitude to the producers of their shows. Recognizing their power, their investment and their rights of hire and fire, company members will always be scrupulously polite – and even ingratiating – towards the money men. They will constantly assert how honoured they are to be part of such a prestigious production.

But when the producers are not in the room, the actors' attitudes to them are rather different. Any complaints about the circumstances in which they're working do, ultimately, have to be placed at the door of the production company. If the rehearsal period is too short, if the set design is too tacky, if the costumes 'look like they've come from the Oxfam shop', if the cast are not allocated enough complimentary tickets for their friends, then the same organization is to blame. Above all, if the actors think they are not being paid enough – and all actors always think they're not being paid enough – then it's the producers' fault.

So, when Justin Grover said that there were no producers at his birthday party, he was using a subtle bonding technique with the rest of the company. It was the snigger of schoolboys behind the bike sheds, exchanging insults about their teachers. Charles was surprised that Justin had made the announcement so baldly. It suggested a slight relaxation of his habitual self-restraint. Charles wondered whether a celebratory bottle of birthday champagne had already been downed in the Number One dressing room before the party proper started.

He found it bizarre, observing the proceedings from the high moral ground of sobriety. Having opted for sparkling water when first offered a drink, he felt he couldn't go back on the route he had chosen, though watching the rest of the company down Justin Grover's champagne was a kind of agony. On the other hand, he did find not drinking made his observation of those around him more acute.

Kell, he noticed, was also on the sparkling water. Realizing he'd never mentioned that he'd followed up on TAUT, he moved across and thanked her for the introduction to the set-up.

'No problem. I hope you're finding it useful.'

'Intriguing, anyway.'

She looked down at his glass. 'Seems to be working.'

He looked at hers. 'Takes one to know one. We still haven't had one of those late-night drinking sessions you promised me.'

'No, I'm actually off the booze completely now.'

'Congratulations. All done by willpower?'

'Willpower, and a bit of help.'

'Oh?'

'I'm giving Alcoholics Anonymous another try,' said Kell, as she moved across the room to join Tod Singer. Who was also on the sparkling water.

Charles took a sip from his glass. It'd never replace the real thing. He also found – something seeming to add insult to injury – that evenings spent drinking sparkling water meant he had to get up to pee in the night more times than he used to on the booze. It was a very unfair world in which virtue was so shabbily rewarded.

He looked round the room. A group of sycophantic actors were roaring with laughter at Justin Grover's imitations of Sir Ian McKellen. With them was Seamus Milligan, looking, as ever, slightly aloof from the action. Charles wandered across to join him.

'Were you in tonight?' he asked, and Seamus nodded. 'Pleased with it?'

'The bits that are usually good were good. The bits that weren't right still aren't right.'

'Oh, I thought the show was settling down rather well.'

'Typical bloody actor's reaction, Charles. So long as the bit you're in is all right, you don't bother about what's happening in the rest of the show.'

'I'm not sure that's fair.'

'Really? When did you last see the whole show?'

'Well, I . . . Obviously, being backstage, it's difficult for me to—'

'Of course it is. Well, I'm out front and I see everything. So, I can judge where the play sags and needs picking up. And the big sag is always when The Girl describes the rape.'

'I thought Imogen was—'

'The way Imogen plays that, it's like she's complaining that some man put his hand on her knee, not like her entire personality has been violated. She's not an actress, Imogen, she's just a Barbie doll. Liddy used to bring some depth to that scene, now it's shallow as hell.'

Charles felt he ought to show a bit of company solidarity. 'Liddy was a very good actress, but I think—'

'Liddy was more than a "very good" actress. She was a bloody great actress!' Charles got the impression that the writer had also been hitting the booze that evening, but he was less surprised than he had been with Justin Grover. 'Liddy Max's death,' Seamus continued, 'was not only a tragic personal loss, but it deprived British theatre of someone who could have been its greatest star!'

Charles looked around, slightly embarrassed, but the rest of the company were too involved in their own conversations to take any notice of this outburst.

'And now,' said Seamus Milligan, 'the part of The Girl – that wonderful part – is being performed by someone who'd hardly pass muster in a primary school Nativity play.'

Nita Glaze had just detached herself from one of the groups and the writer grabbed hold of her as she crossed the room. 'Nita, we've got to do some more work on that rape scene.'

'Seamus, the show has been running for weeks. I'm not in the business of doing any more rehearsal at this stage.'

'But have you seen how that girl Imogen is playing it?'

'My assistant director is now keeping an eye on the show,' Nita Glaze responded with some *hauteur*. 'If you have any points to raise, raise them with him or the production manager.'

'Oh, I see, you've moved on to something new, have you?'

'As it happens, I have.'

'West End?'

'Yes,' Nita replied with some force. 'I'm currently prepping a new show that's going into the Haymarket in March. And now, if you'll excuse me, I need to refresh my drink.' And she moved away.

'So do I,' mumbled Seamus Milligan, making for a champagne bottle as far away as possible from the one Nita was approaching.

Charles emptied his sparkling water glass, but felt too dispirited to top it up with more of the same. There were those night-time pees to think of, apart from anything else. The temptation to pick up a glass of champagne was as strong as ever, but he resisted it.

So, he thought, things have worked out well for Nita Glaze. As he had predicted, the policy of zipping her lip and doing what she was told by Justin Grover had paid off. Her credit on one West End show had immediately led to her being offered a job on another. And in that one, Nita Glaze might be able to impose something of her own vision on the proceedings.

Charles never had found out the reasons for her conflict with Liddy Max in the early days of rehearsal. Certainly, Nita had seemed a lot happier with Imogen Whittaker in the role of The Girl, but to think that the director might have had any responsibility for Liddy's death – well, it just didn't make sense.

Charles found, anyway, that he was thinking much less about the departure of Liddy . . . and of Gideon. Maybe there were some investigations which would never reveal their secrets. He found these days he was much more interested in what was going on at Gower House, and the possibility that he really might be able to exert control over his drinking.

Not wanting to look conspicuously on his own, Charles moved across to where Imogen Whittaker was talking to Grant Yeoell. Her red hair looked dazzling – she must have had time to shower and wash it after removing The Girl's blonde wig. In her eyes was the annoying sparkle that being in the presence of Wulf from *Vandals and Visigoths* seemed to induce in every member of her gender.

'Not a bad show tonight,' was the uncontroversial gambit with which Charles shoehorned himself into the conversation.

'I never know how it's gone,' said Grant. 'Every show seems the same to me.'

Maybe, thought Charles, that's because you give the same

performance every time. Wooden and dull. Unfortunately, the thought reminded him of an old review of his own work. ('To say Charles Paris was wooden would have been an insult to forests.' *Hexham Courant.*)

'Exactly like when we're shooting *Vandals and Visigoths*,' Grant Yeoell continued. 'I do however many takes the director asks me to.' A great many, I'm sure, till they get something usable, was Charles's vindictive thought, as Grant went on, 'I never know why he thinks one take is better than another.'

'They say movies are made in the editing suite,' said Imogen, with the wistfulness of someone who wished she was part of that world.

'Yes, that's where they dub on the performances,' observed Charles. It was a rather crass line, he realized, but Grant Yeoell showed no signs of recognizing it as an insult.

They were joined by Justin Grover, who cast a bonhomous arm over each of the men's shoulders. 'So, what's going on here?' he asked. 'Both of you chatting up the lovely Immy?'

'Having a chat to, rather than chatting up,' Charles responded blandly, feeling even more convinced that Justin had had a bit too much to drink. Man-hugs and backslapping weren't behaviours that came naturally to him.

'Oh, and of course, you never need to chat up, do you, Grant?' There was an edge of jealousy in the star's voice. 'With all your groupies lining up outside the stage door every night?'

The tall Adonis chuckled uneasily. He didn't seem sure where this line of conversation was going. And the realization came to Charles, very forcibly, how insecure someone in Grant Yeoell's position might be. Yes, he was a star with an international following, but he wasn't as big a star as Justin Grover. If Justin ran the *Vandals and Visigoths* set-up the way he was running *The Habit of Faith*, then Grant had probably got the part of Wulf on his say-so. And the time might come when the younger man's stature would be big enough for him to build a successful career without his mentor's patronage, but that point had not yet been reached. Grant Yeoell's future depended entirely on keeping on the right side of Justin Grover.

'Word of advice, though,' Justin went on. 'Before you start any action, Grant, do check your groupies' birth certificates. Underage is never good. In the current climate, there are so many things that could ruin an actor's career.'

'Things from the distant past?' Charles suggested.

The look of pure venom that Justin Grover turned on him lasted only a nanosecond before it was replaced by a joshing grin, but it did remind Charles of the questions about the star's past. And what might or might not have gone on in Bridport.

'Even someone as young as Grant here has a past,' said Justin. 'And you never know what's going to crawl out from under a stone, do you? Particularly for someone who's bedded as many thousands of women as you have, eh, Grant?'

'You mustn't believe everything you read in the tabloids,' the younger actor replied smoothly. He was still uncomfortable, but his natural cockiness was beginning to reassert itself.

'The trouble is,' said Justin, 'the more sex one has, the more one gets bored with it. Don't you find that?' He turned suddenly to the girl. 'Do *you* find that, Imogen?'

She looked thrown for a moment, but quickly regained her stability. Her life as an actress had thickened her skin against attacks of male banter, and her normal riposte would probably have been crude and crushing. But she was not in a normal situation. Justin Grover was not only the star of her current show, he was also a potential conduit to other, more prestigious and lucrative shows.

Judiciously, she replied, 'I'm glad to say, I haven't got to the point where I'm bored with sex.'

'Lucky you,' said Justin Grover. 'And lucky men with whom you share not being bored.'

Yes, thought Charles, he definitely *is* pissed. He wouldn't normally be so crass.

'But your case, Grant,' Justin went on, 'is rather different, isn't it?'

'I don't know what you mean.' The nervousness was back in the reply.

'Ooh, you're not going to deny it now, are you? What you told me on location in Arizona?'

'What did I tell you?' Grant Yeoell faltered.

'You said . . . let me make sure I get the words right . . . "I'm so bored with normal sex that these days I can only get it up if I'm dressed in costume."'

SEVENTEEN

By chance, Charles left the party at the same time as Grant Yeoell. As they walked cautiously down the steep stairs, he dared to ask, 'Was Liddy Max among your conquests, Grant?'

'I don't think of them as "conquests",' came the reply. 'Just a very pleasant perk of the job I do.' This wasn't spoken boastfully, simply as a matter of fact.

'Going back to Liddy . . .'

'Yes.'

'Did you make love to her?'

Charles was expecting some kind of evasive answer, but he got a direct, 'Yes.'

'On the day she died?'

Again, 'Yes.' Then, 'But I didn't know she was going to die, did I?'

'I'm surprised you're telling me this so openly.'

'Why?'

'Well, her death was suspicious, and if you were making love to her only hours before . . .'

'You mean the police might be interested?'

'Yes.'

'They were. So, I told them what happened.'

'And weren't they suspicious that you might have killed her?'

'They might have been, except that Liddy had made a phone call on her mobile after I left. And then someone witnessed me leaving the theatre.'

'Who?'

'A girl.'

'One of your groupies?'

'I do wish you and Justin would stop using that word. It's very dated. I prefer to think of the girls as "fans". Also, Justin keeps implying that I go to bed with all of them. Which I don't. Most are underage, anyway. Just kids full of excess adolescent emotion that they have to focus somewhere. Last time I did a show in the West End, there was one girl who turned up every night of the entire run.

Called Shelley. Full marks for effort, I suppose.' He shrugged. 'Presumably she got some kind of strange kick out of doing it.'

'Going back to that Monday night – how did the girl at the stage door know you were in the theatre?'

'She'd seen me go in.'

'When did you speak to the police?'

'The day after Liddy died.'

The same day they had interviewed Charles; the day when he had been almost immobilized by his hangover. 'Have you heard from them again?'

'No.'

'So, you wouldn't know how they thought Liddy died?'

'I assume they thought what everyone else thought.'

'Which was?'

'Oh, come on, Charles. What has everyone been saying backstage?'

Charles genuinely didn't know. He had been so preoccupied with his own assumption of murder that he hadn't really listened to the company consensus. 'What have they been saying?'

'That it was an accident. Liddy tripped. The habit she was wearing was much too big for her.'

'And you don't feel any guilt about her death?'

'Why should I? I'm very sorry the poor girl died, obviously. I quite liked her.' The way he said this didn't suggest there had been much love involved in their coupling. 'But her death wasn't my fault.'

'Weren't you the one who suggested you should dress up in the monks' habits?'

There was an infinitesimal pause before Grant replied, 'No, that was her idea. Liddy Max had surprisingly kinky tastes, you know.'

'And who else has kinky tastes?' asked Charles.

'Sorry?'

'Are you aware of someone in the company who's a voyeur?'

Grant Yeoell turned his infinitely handsome, infinitely blank, face towards Charles, and said, 'No', in a puzzled manner that meant he had to be telling the truth. It seemed he had not known that he and Liddy had been performing for the cameras.

The two had reached the stage door. They handed in their keys to Wallace, who wished them a cheery good night from the cubby-hole which he now seemed to have inhabited forever. Gideon had just melted away into blankness.

As Grant Yeoell went out into the after-midnight darkness, a pair of squealing teenage girls rushed towards him.

'It is working. To some extent.'

'Really, Charles?' Long experience justified the scepticism in Frances's voice.

'Yes.'

'So how many days this week have you done without booze?'

'Three.'

'That's good.' She sounded impressed. 'And are you finding it easy?'

'No. Bloody hard.'

'Keep at it.'

'I will. And . . . how about us meeting up?'

'I'm going down to Juliet and Miles's for Sunday lunch. I don't know if you fancy—?'

'I don't think so.' The prospect of his son-in-law pontificating on his abstinence was not one he relished. 'I'd rather see you on your own.'

'Yes, I'd like that.'

'When?' he asked eagerly.

'When you're off the booze, Charles.'

Playing the part of Brother Benedict, The Monk Who Just Listened To All Of The Other Monks Who Maundered On In Long Speeches About Their Own Internal Conflicts, inevitably had its longueurs. While Abbot Ambrose was hardly off the stage for the duration of *The Habit of Faith* (surprise, surprise), the rest of the cast had to spend long periods in their dressing rooms.

Some were very organized about this. There was a foursome who gathered in Tod Singer's dressing room during the second act to play Bridge, and could almost always fit in a rubber (while onstage Abbot Ambrose and The Girl endlessly discussed sex and guilt), before they had to reappear for the last scene.

Charles had two habitual ways of whiling away time in his dressing room. One, which he no longer practised – though not practising it constantly tested his resources of willpower – involved a bottle of Bell's. The other was *The Times* crossword. But on the Friday, the day after Justin Grover's birthday party, there had been a particularly easy puzzle, which he'd finished over a sandwich at lunchtime. So, having forgotten to bring a book with him, Charles had no alternative, in his dressing room that evening, but to sit and think.

He thought first about that day's 'Weekend Group' session at Gower House. Erica had been there to direct the discussion when required, but as usual in those Friday meetings, the participants had done most of the work themselves. Once again, Charles had been impressed by the honesty and humour on display. Though the make-up of the attendance shifted from week to week, there were now enough people he knew for him to join in the general banter. And he had felt the genuine warmth which greeted his announcement of the small triumph of not drinking at Justin's birthday party. He couldn't say what in the regime was working, but he was beginning to feel that getting off the booze was not a total impossibility. Just hang on in there.

Then his mind moved on to the crimes at the Duke of Kent's Theatre.

Grant Yeoell's openness about being Liddy Max's sexual partner had rather thrown him. Charles had expected some form of denial or cover-up, but had got neither. Grant had seemed to regard the encounter as just another notch on wherever he cut his many notches. Another significant fact was that he hadn't asked how Charles knew about him and Liddy. That suggested the information was common knowledge in *The Habit of Faith* company. Charles had just missed out on the news.

The other question that kept recurring to him was the identity of the voyeur for whom the spy camera had been set up in Liddy's dressing room. There was no doubt that Gideon had planted the device, but had it been for his own benefit? He was the kind of person who would fit the popular *Daily Mail* profile of a voyeur. And when he and Charles had met in the pub the day after Liddy's death, Gideon had spoken of having 'very secret secrets'. It must have been him.

And yet Charles's doubt persisted. He was still drawn to the idea that Gideon had been following someone else's orders.

And he also suspected that that someone had helped Gideon consume all the vodka that caused his death. In fact, that Gideon had been murdered.

*   *   *

A conversation with Kell confirmed that most of the *Habit* company did now know about Gideon and Liddy's encounter. But nobody else knew – or had admitted to knowing – that the action had been filmed.

Each night on his walk from the tube to the Duke of Kent's, Charles looked out for Baz. But Gideon's companion seemed to have vanished from the face of the earth as effectively as Gideon himself.

The following Thursday, the word on the flipchart at Gower House was 'Obstacles', and Ricky led a discussion about the hurdles that lay across the route to freedom from addiction. At the beginning of the session he had introduced a tall, grey-haired man to the group. 'This is Trevor, who's going to sit in this afternoon as an observer. He fully understands about the confidentiality issues here at Gower House, so don't worry about talking freely.'

Charles thought the man looked vaguely familiar, but soon forgot his presence as the discussion developed.

After all the participants had done their 'check-outs', assessing their moods at the end of the session, there were a few 'See you tomorrows' as they all set off in their different directions. But just as he was leaving the room, Charles was stopped by the tall newcomer.

'You're Charles Paris, aren't you?'

As soon as Trevor mentioned the movie, Charles knew exactly who he was. In fact, given how small his contributions had been to the film industry, he should have got there quicker. Trevor Race had directed one of Charles's few appearances on the silver screen. The film had been one of those 'state of the nation' pieces of the 1980s. Overtly political, *Doorstep Sandwiches* had been an excoriating attack on the devastation wreaked by the Thatcher government, seen through the travails of a young couple in Doncaster. Charles Paris had taken on the minuscule role of the second bailiff, whose impact had been too minor to garner any press reviews.

Indeed, very little of his film work had ever been reviewed. The only notice he recollected was for an experimental movie called *Onion Braids*, written and directed by an Oxford contemporary soon after they left the university. ('Charles Paris wandered through the action with the shell-shocked expression of someone who hadn't yet recovered from reading the script for the first time.' *Sight and Sound.*) The director, recognizing the wrong direction he had taken in life, quickly joined the civil service, where he was still in the Department of Work and Pensions, accumulating a very large pension of his own and likely soon to receive a knighthood. Less shrewd, Charles Paris had continued to pursue a career in the theatre.

Trevor Race had led Charles up to a well-appointed flat on the top floor of Gower House. From the kitchen, where he was tending the coffee-maker, could be seen the wealthy roofs of Finchley.

'So, Trevor,' asked Charles, 'how do you come to be involved in TAUT? Are you on the staff?'

'Good Lord, no. I'm still making movies.'

Charles gave himself a black mark. He should have known that.

'No,' Trevor went on, 'I started TAUT.'

'Sorry?'

'I set up the charity.' He gestured round the room. 'This is my house.'

'Gower House is yours?'

'Yes. I used to live here. Still use this flat sometimes when I'm in London. Which isn't very often.'

'Where are you the rest of the time?'

'Wherever the current movie's being shot. I do have a villa on Mykonos, where I go between projects. But I never spend long there.'

'So why did you set up TAUT?'

'Ah. You don't know what it stands for, do you?'

'No. I keep meaning to ask one of the staff here, but never get round to it.'

'Right. Did you know an actor called Alan Unsworth?'

'I may have heard the name.'

'Alan was in *Doorstep Sandwiches*.' There was a note of reproof in the voice.

'Well, perhaps I wasn't in any scenes with him.'

'You were.' The tartness was now unmistakable. 'Alan played the neighbour who tried to stop you and the other bailiff from breaking down the door.'

'Oh yes, of course, I remember,' Charles lied.

'He was a very good actor, Alan.'

'I remember being impressed,' Charles lied further.

'He was also the love of my life.'

There was a silence. Charles wasn't quite sure of the correct response to a statement like that.

'But Alan,' Trevor went on, 'had a kamikaze element in his personality. He kept doing stupid things. That was all right when he was on his own, bouncing in and out of relationships, never knowing what he really wanted in life. But after we got together . . . we had stability, we loved each other, we had no money worries . . . and he still had this urge to break it all.'

'Drink?' Charles suggested.

'Oh yes. Drink.' Trevor Race again gestured around the room. 'Hence TAUT. The Alan Unsworth Trust, that's what it stands for. A memorial to him. Not the memorial I would wish for, but . . . maybe better than nothing.'

'I'm certainly appreciating what's going on here.'

'Good. The staff are brilliant. When I decided to set TAUT up, I wanted to do it properly. Everyone fully qualified. I did a lot of research to get the right people. I didn't know much about the mechanics of addiction, until it was too late. But after Alan died, I made it my business to find out stuff. I did a lot of research into various different approaches, and hired the people who seemed to be getting the best results. I know the TAUT system doesn't work for everyone, but if it does for even one person, then I guess my efforts haven't been wasted.'

'I've noticed that TAUT deals with all kinds of addictions. Was Alan also into drugs?'

'Alan never did drugs,' came the sharp response.

'And you finance the whole thing yourself, do you, Trevor?'

The tall man shrugged. 'Yes. There's a lot of money to be made in the film industry. I've made a great deal. And there's nothing I want to spend it on. I travel all the time for work, so there's not much pleasure for me in exotic holidays. I've got as much property as I need. Flashy cars, ridiculously priced watches, I don't want them.' He was expressing the familiar dilemma of the 'champagne Socialist'. Trevor Race had set out on an artistic course which defended the interests of the 'have-nots' against the depredations of the 'haves'. And by doing so, he had accumulated so much money that he could no longer pretend not to be a 'have'.

'It would be different, of course, if Alan was still alive. Travelling with him was something else. I never knew what was going to happen next. But travelling on my own . . . doing anything on my own . . .' His eyes misted over. 'Things have changed so much. There are changes that Alan will never see. The two of us could actually be *married* now, for God's sake! But that'll never happen. So much'll never happen.

'I still keep asking myself what more I could have done. Towards the end I stopped working – I gave up a couple of very lucrative movies just to look after Alan. I tried to monitor him every hour of the day and night, see that no booze got into the house. But alcoholics are devious – I don't need to tell you that, Charles. Whatever precautions I took, he still managed to smuggle the stuff in. Alan really did have a death wish. So, I suppose . . . he got what he wanted.'

There was a long pause before Trevor pulled himself together, and asked, 'Is it the booze with you, Charles? Is that why you're here?'

'Yes.'

'No drugs?'

'No.'

'That's good. And how're you going on the road to total abstinence?'

Charles still wasn't entirely convinced that was the road he wanted to be on, but he just said, 'OK.'

'When did you last work?'

Unusually, he was able to reply, 'I'm working at the moment.'

'Good. I'm sorry, I'd kind of assumed that you couldn't get any work, because of your problem with the booze.'

Before he'd started attending Gower House, Charles's instant reaction would have been, 'I'm not that bad!' He would have separated himself from the people who lost jobs and houses and had their children taken into care, but now he was less condemning. He and the others, they all had the same problem. It was just a matter of degree.

'What are you doing?' asked Trevor.

'Play at the Duke of Kent's. *The Habit of Faith.*'

Trevor Race shook his head. 'Sorry, I've been away so much, I'm not up with West End theatre. Don't know anything about it.'

'New play set in a monastery.'

'Oh God.'

'Vehicle for Justin Grover.'

'Really? One of those actors who works it all out himself, doesn't like the intervention of a director.'

'You've described him perfectly.'

'God, I can't stand working with people like that! Fortunately, I very rarely have to. Got to the point in my career where I have a veto on casting. But making movies is such a technical exercise, the actors must respect the director's skills, or the whole thing implodes.'

'So, when did you work with him?'

'I never have, thank the Lord. But I've heard a lot about him. One of my oldest friends worked with Justin Grover right at the beginning of his career. When he was just one of any number of interchangeable actors, fresh out of drama school. Long before he would bestride the world as Sigismund the Strong.'

'What was your friend's name?'

'Damian Grantchester. He used to run the theatre in Bridport.'

EIGHTEEN

The most famous retirement home for members of the acting profession is Denville Hall in Northwood, Middlesex. Damian Grantchester wasn't in that one, but it was clear from the way Charles was greeted by the garrulous lady on reception that the home in Dorking also had strong theatrical ties.

'Yes, we got your message, Mr Paris. Damian will be delighted to see you. He loves talking over old times with his theatre chums. And the weekends can be quite long for him if he has no visitors.'

'I can't stay long, I'm afraid. Saturday matinee.'

'Yes, of course. You're in the play at the Duke of Kent's, aren't you?' She was clearly well informed about current theatre. 'I recognized your name when I got the message.'

'Oh yes?' said Charles, with the actor's hunger for validation.

But the receptionist didn't go on to praise his performances. She just asked, 'Did you work with Damian?'

'A long time ago.'

'Everything's a long time ago when you get to our age, Mr Paris,' she said, prompting him to wonder if he did actually look as old as she did. 'Oh, and I can't keep on calling you "Mr Paris". May I call you "Charles"?'

'Please do.'

'Damian's in the conservatory, Charles. You get a lovely view of the garden from there.'

It was a lovely view. The double-glazed conservatory was toasty warm like the rest of the building, insulated from the frosted world outside.

If he hadn't known who it was, Charles would not have recognized Damian Grantchester. Back in Bridport days, the director had been pencil-thin and sharp-featured, with shoulder-length black hair, a coiled-up spring of nervous energy. He had the kind of body you could never imagine turning to fat.

And yet that is what time had achieved. Damian was not fat on the scale of Gideon, but his flesh did seem to be spilling out from the wicker armchair in which he sat. He was dressed in burgundy elephant-cord trousers, a thick navy-blue cardigan done up with leather toggles, and his signature paisley cravat at the neck. His swollen feet were almost contained in ugly black shoes with Velcro strapping. The hair was still worn long, but now white and very sparse. The shape of his shining cranium was clear through the wisps.

Yet, the longer he spent with him, the more Charles recognized of the old Damian Grantchester. The eyes still flashed with the same fire. The characteristic hand gestures, though now slower, hadn't changed. And the familiar waspish wit had not lost its sting.

Charles had forgotten how much Damian Grantchester relished gossip. And gossip of a particularly vicious kind. It soon became clear that, although tucked away in a care home in Dorking, Damian kept up with his theatrical contacts. His talk was constantly punctuated with sentences beginning, 'I was on the phone only yesterday to so-and-so and he told me this amazing rumour about . . .' The telephone was clearly his main lifeline. He was of too old a generation to have embraced email.

'And I got your message, Charles, but I can't remember who it was who put you in touch with me.'

'Trevor Race.'

'Oh yes. Dear Trevor. Always comes to see me when he's in the country. Came down here for lunch last Sunday. Still in pretty good nick, isn't he?'

'Looks very well, yes.'

'You cannot believe how beautiful Trev was as a young man. Not just attractive – beautiful. He and I had a little flurry of fun way back then. Nothing too serious, though I think that was always what he was looking for. And then, of course, later he met Alan. Did you ever know Alan?'

'No.'

'Lovely boy too. But very naughty.'

'The booze?'

'Well, the booze was part of it, but there was lots of other stuff. Drugs, certainly.'

'Trevor told me that Alan never used drugs.'

'Well, maybe that's what dear Trev wanted to believe. I think he knew. He must've known. Everyone else in the business knew.

'The other thing, of course, was that Alan was pathologically unfaithful. Always getting inside other people's trousers. And some pretty unsavoury trousers, too. Rent boys, real riff-raff. Trev was always digging him out of some mess or another, paying off yet another debt Alan had incurred. He tried to keep an eye on Alan by casting him in every movie he made, but the boy usually found someone to be unfaithful with on location. Trev had this fantasy of the two of them settling down as a couple, but that was never going to be Alan's way.'

Charles reflected that maybe Trevor Race had posthumously beatified his lover. His regret at Alan not having lived long enough for them to be legally married may not have taken into account the personality he had been dealing with.

It was as if Damian Grantchester was reading his thoughts, because he said, 'Trevor made a very big deal of it when Alan died. Kept going on about how it was the great love of his life, turned this rather shifty character, only one step up from a rent boy, into a plaster saint. If my sources are correct – and they usually are – Trev hasn't been to bed with anyone else since Alan died. Story goes he's even rejected the offers of sexual favours from aspiring actors, which is frankly amazing, because those are reckoned to be one of the perks of being a director.' The old man chuckled in fond recollection. 'And Trev's turned that lovely house of his in Finchley to some sort of shrine to Alan. A therapy centre, is it?'

'Something like that, I believe,' said Charles, unaccountably unwilling to admit how he and Trevor Race had met.

'Of course,' Damian went on, 'you were quite good-looking back in the Bridport days, Charles. I could have fancied you back then, you know. But men were never your thing, were they?'

'Sorry.'

'Oh, Charles.' The old man sighed. 'You don't know what you're missing.'

Here was an opportunity to close in on the reason for his visit to Dorking. Charles said, 'I was thinking back to when I worked for you in Bridport.'

'Oh, surely, love, you don't say that. You didn't work *for* me. We worked *together*. At the Imperial we were part of an *ensemble*, weren't we?' His emphasis pointed up the pretentiousness of the word. 'Or had we got beyond all that *ensemble* nonsense by then?'

'Well, we weren't an *ensemble* in the sense that we started every morning with an hour of improvisation to *home in* on our characters.'

'Too right we weren't. No time for that sort of farting about. We had shows to put on.'

'Yes, I was thinking back to your production of *Hamlet* . . .'

'Ah yes. A bit highbrow for the good burghers of Bridport. They always preferred a good old Agatha Christie to your Shakespeare. Thank God *Hamlet* was an A-level set text that year. Without the school parties we wouldn't have broken even.' A glow of nostalgia suffused the old director's features. 'And do you remember that lovely boy who played Hamlet?'

'I don't remember his name. I remember what he looked like.'

'So do I! Beautiful blond hair. Natural too, not a bottle job like Larry Olivier in the movie. Looked properly Nordic, as Hamlet should. Richard Frail, that was the boy's name. I thought he really had potential. His Hamlet was the perfect mix of the introvert and the extrovert. I thought he'd go all the way. Last thing I heard he was selling insurance in Salford. Dame Theatre can be a cruel mistress.' Damian turned his bright eyes on Charles. 'And you gave your Rosencrantz, didn't you, you clever boy?'

'Or was it Guildenstern?'

'No, you were definitely Rosencrantz. The Guildenstern was a boy I regard as the luckiest actor in the world. Justin Grover.'

'That's right.'

'Mind you, he wasn't bad-looking back then. I wouldn't have kicked either of you out of bed. Even nurtured these daydreams – a threesome with Rosencrantz and Guildenstern. But I suppose every director of *Hamlet* has fantasies like that, don't they?'

Charles didn't take issue with this arguable assertion. Instead, he said, 'Going back to Justin . . .'

'Yes. Strange who the gods pick out for special treatment, isn't it? Justin Grover, perfectly adequate actor, a bit too technical for my taste. And with a few rather annoying quirks.'

'Do you remember the Buddhist chanting?' asked Charles.

'Oh, God, yes. What a poseur he was! And probably still is.'

'I can confirm that.'

'Are you in touch with the dear boy?'

'I'm working with him.'

'Well, heavens to Betsy! In an *ensemble*?'

'Justin keeps referring to it as an *ensemble*, but of course it's nothing of the sort. Anything Justin's involved in is basically all about him.'

'I know the show you're talking about, read the reviews. The monkfest! A lot of men in habits wanking about at the Duke of Kent's?'

'Exactly that, Damian. And there's another cast member who worked with you at Bridport. Tod Singer.'

'God, I remember him. The piss artist to end all piss artists.'

'Now completely dry. A devotee of Alcoholics Anonymous.'

The old man cupped his hands around his face in mock-horror. 'How ghastly! In a changing world, there are so few certainties one can cling on to. Mind you, Charles, as I recall, you were not an enemy of the bottle. I hope you haven't joined Tod on that oh-so-dispiriting wagon.'

It wasn't the moment to chronicle his own journey on the road to abstinence, so Charles just said, 'I still enjoy a drink.' Which remained distressingly true.

'Thank the Lord for that. Strange how the theatre works, though, isn't it? From the production of *Hamlet*, I wouldn't have said any of the cast was going to make it at any major level—' Charles did not allow himself to be put down by the implied insult – 'except for that boy Richard Frail. I thought he was destined to go right to the top. Which just goes to show how little I know. Hamlet is now selling insurance in Salford, and Guildenstern – an actor of minimal talent and some rather unwholesome habits – becomes a global superstar. I think anyone entering the theatre should be firmly told that it is not a business in which fairness plays any part at all.'

'That's true,' Charles agreed glumly.

'All the observations, incidentally, Charles, are in my book.'

'Which book is this?'

'I've written a memoir. Called *Beginners, Please*. Lots in it about my time at the Imperial.'

'Great. Where can I get hold of a copy?'

'Ah. Sadly, you may have to wait awhile for that. The book is not yet in print. It has done the rounds of the publishing houses, but none of them is interested in the reminiscences of a theatre director of the third rank.' Charles felt that he ought to perhaps remonstrate, but, then again, Damian Grantchester's self-assessment was probably accurate. 'If I were a star – or if I'd slept with enough stars – no doubt the reaction would be different. *Beginners, Please* would even now be storming the bestsellers' lists. In my current situation, though, I can't give myself away with soap.

'I have a friend who comes to visit me. She works in publishing, and she's going to see if she can place the book somewhere. But she's my last hope. If she can't get a publishing deal, then I'm afraid all my carefully collected dirt will go to the grave with me. "Earth to earth, ashes to ashes", not forgetting "dirt to dirt".' The old man sighed. 'Sorry, I've gone all "sicklied o'er with the pale cast of thought".'

Charles respected a moment of silence, before moving on. 'You said Justin had . . . "some rather unwholesome habits"?'

'Yes. I'm surprised you weren't aware of them. You two shared a dressing room, didn't you?'

'Yes. Though I spent as little time there as I could politely get away with.'

'The Buddhist chanting got on your nerves?'

'Yes, and a few other irritating habits. When I was offstage – which, if you're playing Rosencrantz, is most of the evening – I generally hung around the Green Room.'

'No, you didn't, Charles. We've covered this already. You know full well that you spent all your time offstage inside the knickers of our Gertrude. Didn't you?'

'Well . . .' The monosyllable contained equal measures of shame and pride. Oh, Damian would know the name of the actress playing Gertrude.

But before Charles had a chance to ask the question, the director went on, 'By not being in the dressing room, you were probably doing Justin a favour.'

'Oh?'

'Allowing him to pursue his little hobby.'

'Little hobby?'

'After the *Hamlet* production finished, there was some mainte-nance work scheduled for all the Imperial dressing rooms. And in the one you shared with Justin, the workmen found a hole had been drilled through the wall. They called me to have a look. I remember, I was giving the guy who'd written the next show a guided tour of the theatre, and we went though and had a look. The hole had been drilled through into the next dressing room.'

'I can't remember who would have been in—'

'Ophelia.'

'Very pretty girl, whose name escapes me.'

'Eve Blanche. Anyway, there was a spy-hole from your dressing room, through which the poor kid could be watched, presumably when she was changing into costume . . . or doing whatever else she got up to in the privacy of her dressing room. Well, I knew you wouldn't be responsible for drilling that hole, Charles.'

'Thank you.' It was a kind of compliment.

'You were too busy, up to no good inside Gertrude's knickers.' Perhaps not such a compliment, after all.

'No, it was Justin Grover. I rang him straight after the hole had been found. He denied it, of course. But I followed up with a call to our Ophelia. She said Justin had come on to her and said things about her body which suggested he'd seen her naked. Which, so far as she knew, he hadn't.

'There's no doubt about it, Charles. Justin Grover was a Peeping Tom.'

NINETEEN

Charles cornered Grant Yeoell in his dressing room between the matinee and the evening performances. The tall actor seemed deeply involved in communing with his tablet.

'Sorry, have you got a moment, Grant?'

'Yes. Could do with a break. It's a full-time job keeping up with my Twitter followers.'

Charles wasn't entirely sure he knew what that meant, but he did know it was not a problem that he had.

'It's going back to Liddy Max . . .'

Grant let out an exasperated sigh. 'We've talked about this already, Charles. Yes, we made love, dressed in monks' habits. And that would have been the end of it . . . but for the fact that Liddy fell down the stairs and died the same evening.'

'So, it was going to be a one-off? No plans for an ongoing relationship?'

'No,' said Grant, as if the idea were completely incongruous.

'And did Liddy know that was the deal too?'

'I've no idea. I assumed so.'

'You didn't think that she might have been in love with you?'

A grimace crossed the perfect features. 'It wasn't something I thought about. I think love is a woman's construct. Men feel differently. My view is that, if someone wants me to make love to them, assuming they're attractive – well, I'm up for it.'

'I spoke to Liddy's husband . . .'

'I didn't know she had a husband.'

'Well, she did. Called Derek. He said she was obsessed with her career.'

'True of a lot of actors.'

'He also said she was hoping being in *Habit* might lead to her getting a part in a *Vandals and Visigoths* movie.'

'I wouldn't have thought that was very likely to happen.'

'No, but clearly she thought it was. Being in a play with Justin Grover, and with you – well, she thought it might raise her chances.'

'As I say, I wouldn't have thought it likely. Justin does sometimes recommend actors to the *Vandals* producers, but I've never heard him mention Liddy in that context.'

'And what about you?'

'What about me? I wasn't in the movies on Justin's say-so. The casting directors picked me out from some modelling shoots I'd done.'

Charles couldn't have imagined Grant would have been spotted doing anything that involved acting. But he went on, 'No, what I meant was: do you think Liddy thought you might have some influence with the producers? Do you think that was why she was so ready to have sex with you?'

'I suppose it's possible.' He didn't sound that interested. 'I thought it was just because she fancied me.' Once again, he spoke as though being fatally attractive to women was a rather tiresome occupational hazard. 'But if she did think I had any influence with the producers, then she was barking up the wrong tree. Justin's the one who can make things happen there, not me. The whole production now works completely on his say-so. Everyone always does what Justin wants.'

Charles suddenly had a new idea. 'Including you?'

'What do you mean?'

'Do you always do what Justin wants?'

'I work with him a lot. Obviously on the *Vandals and Visigoths* movies, now on this. He's the star. Nobody argues about that. But he can be surprisingly generous to other cast members.'

'That wasn't what I meant. If Justin asked you to do something, would you do it?'

'It depends what it—'

'Because presumably he has the power to fire as well as hire? So, it would pay to keep on the right side of him?'

Grant Yeoell conceded that that was the case.

'And has Justin ever suggested that you should come on to some woman?'

'Well . . .'

'You know, said, "That one definitely fancies you. You'd be well in there", that kind of thing?'

'He may have said things like that. But it's just – what's the current expression? – "locker room talk".'

'And did Justin suggest to you that Liddy Max might be . . . susceptible to your charms? That she might be a potential target for you?'

Grant Yeoell turned his beautiful, expressionless eyes on Charles, and said, 'Yes.'

Kell handed the spy camera across without asking any questions.

'Is Justin about?' asked Charles. 'Or does he go out between the shows?'

'He's in his dressing room. Tends to put his feet up, after the *emotional strain* of giving of himself in the matinee.' She caught in the two words some essence of the star's preciousness, the quality he had displayed when, all those weeks before, he'd asked the company to 'breathe in the atmosphere' of the Duke of Kent's Theatre.

Kell looked straight at Charles. Her eyes had all the acuteness that Grant Yeoell's lacked. 'So, you reckon the spy camera was for Justin's benefit?'

'Beginning to look that way.'

She nodded slowly. 'That would figure.'

'What do you mean? Do you know something?'

'You hear a lot round the stage management grapevine.'

'I'm sure you do.'

'Some of it's just spiteful gossip, but if you hear the same thing enough times . . .'

'No smoke without . . .?'

'Exactly, Charles. So, let's say your suspicions prove to be true – well, there might be people around who could provide corroborating evidence.'

'People you could contact?'

Kell nodded.

There was a long silence after Charles's knock. He thought Justin might be asleep, and was about to go back to his own dressing room when the door opened. Justin looked alert. He had removed his habit, and was dressed in jeans and a casual cardigan.

'Charles. What can I do for you?'

'I hope I'm not disturbing . . .' Though, of course, the purpose of his visit was very definitely to disturb.

'No, please. Come in.'

Justin stood back. Charles hadn't been in this particular Number One dressing room before. It was not only considerably bigger, but also much better decorated and equipped than those of the lowlier company members.

'Take a seat.' Justin Grover gestured broadly. 'Can I get you a coffee or something?'

There was a state-of-the-art Italian machine on a shelf, but Charles demurred.

'So,' said Justin, sitting in an armchair set at an angle to his make-up mirror, 'what can I do for you?'

Charles put the eyeball-shaped spy camera on the low table between them. 'Do you know what that is?'

'No,' Justin replied.

'It's a spy camera.'

'Really? Are you into espionage, Charles?'

'I'm not, no.'

'Well, thank you so much for showing me that. Absolutely fascinating. And now . . .' He pointed to the door. 'I do have another performance today, and Abbot Ambrose is not an untaxing role.'

'Sorry to take up more of your time, Justin,' Charles insisted, 'but I do have more to say about this spy camera.'

'Really?'

'It was set up by Gideon, our late lamented stage doorman.'

'I know who Gideon was. I met him when I was doing a previous show here. Anyway, I always know everyone backstage.'

If Justin was hoping to receive commendation for his magnanimous common touch, he didn't get it. 'Gideon set up the camera to spy on Liddy Max.'

'How he got his sexual gratification is not really of much interest to me, Charles. Particularly now the poor man's dead.'

'It's my view that, when Gideon set up the spy camera, he didn't do it for his own pleasure. He was obeying orders.'

'From whom?'

'Someone in the company.'

Justin Grover shrugged. 'So, we have a voyeur in our midst. Is that really such a surprise in this day and age?'

'After Gideon found Liddy's body . . . you know, the night she died . . . he removed this camera from her dressing room.'

'A very wise precaution, I would imagine, since the police would inevitably be crawling all over the place.'

'The output from this camera could have been viewed by anyone who linked up to it on their computer or tablet or smartphone.'

'How very useful for people who get their kicks from watching actresses change into their costumes.'

'The camera recorded a lot more than that.'

'Oh, did it?'

'It recorded, that same evening, Grant Yeoell making love to Liddy Max.'

There was a silence. For the first time, Charles felt he'd got an unprepared reaction from Justin Grover.

But the moment didn't last long. The customary detached irony was back in the response, 'Well, perhaps we should be grateful that the poor girl's last few hours on earth included some pleasurable activity.'

'I've talked to Grant.'

'I'm glad to hear it. I like to feel we're a happy company, in which everyone talks to everyone else.'

Charles was not going to be put off by this nonchalant stonewalling. 'Grant has told me that on occasions you have suggested women for him to come on to.'

Justin spread his hands wide. 'One likes to help one's co-workers when one can.'

'Grant doesn't need your help in getting women.'

'No, they do rather throw themselves at the poor boy, don't they?'

Charles tried a different tack. 'From the start of this production, I found it interesting how many people involved in *The Habit of Faith* have a connection to the theatre in Bridport.'

'You and me, obviously, doing our immortal double act as Rosencrantz and Guildenstern. Or was it the other way round?'

'Also Tod Singer. And Seamus Milligan, come to that. Don't you find that rather a coincidence?'

A shrug. 'If an actor can't help out an old chum, what has the world of theatre come to, eh?' It was, word for word, exactly the same line which had made Charles feel so patronized at the read-through. Justin looked at him shrewdly, as he went on, 'Why, you don't have a more sinister explanation for my generosity, do you?'

'Interesting times we live in,' Charles observed. 'Particularly in the theatre. Sexual misdemeanours from long ago being brought to light on a daily basis. What's that catch-all expression that keeps coming up? "Inappropriate behaviour." If every time a director had groped a pretty young actress, or an actor had goosed an ASM in the prop store . . . if all of those incidents become retrospectively actionable, where will it all end?'

'Where indeed?' asked Justin. But there was a new caution in his voice.

'I just wondered,' said Charles casually, 'whether getting so many "old chums" from Bridport together in *The Habit of Faith* might be a way of buying our silence.'

'"Buying your silence"? Silence about what?'

'Hm. You remember Damian Grantchester?'

'Of course I do. Camp as a row of teepees. Responsible for our deathless Rosencrantz and Guildenstern double act.'

'Yes.'

'Must be long dead, poor bugger.'

'As it happens, no.'

'Oh?'

'I saw him this morning. In a care home in Dorking.'

'You must give me the address. I'd love to be in touch with the old queen.'

'Yes, you might well.'

'What do you mean by that tone of voice, Charles?'

'I mean you might like to find a way of buying his silence too.' Justin did not respond. 'But you'd be a bit late. Damian has already told me about your . . . well, I guess the phrase is "inappropriate behaviour", in Bridport.'

'What did he say?' The mask of insouciance was off. Justin wanted to know the answer, wanted to know the level of damage that might need limitation.

Charles told him about the hole drilled through the wall into Ophelia's dressing room. He told him about the girl's puzzlement as to Justin's intimate knowledge of her anatomy.

There was a silence. Then Justin Grover asked, 'And do you believe any of this?'

'Yes, I do. And I believe it's related to Liddy Max's death.'

'Hm.' Justin took his time. 'When someone gets to my level of fame, notoriety, whatever you want to call it, a lot of nice things happen, and a lot of unpleasant ones too. The press are savage predators, and nowadays ordinary members of the public on social media are even worse. Anything shabby, anything slightly iffy from your past, is dragged up at every opportunity. Everyone wants a piece of you, and if they get that piece by taking you to court, they regard that as part of the fun.

'So, if some senile old queen in a care home in Dorking claims to recall, through the cobwebs of his memory, that Justin Grover, now known across the world as Sigismund the Strong from *Vandals and Visigoths*, was a Peeping Tom – well, that's just the kind of thing to set up a feeding frenzy.'

'Are you denying his allegation is true?'

'Of course I am, Charles,' said Justin wearily. 'And, what's more, I know why he made it.'

'Oh?'

'It's quite ironic, really, all this talk of "inappropriate behaviour". As you probably remember, Damian Grantchester used to come on to anything in trousers. Always had to ensure you didn't go to have a pee at the same time as he did. He must have made advances to you, surely, Charles?'

'Well, a bit. Rather half-hearted.'

'Let me tell you, in my case, they were far from half-hearted. Damian spent that entire production trying to touch me up. He said it wasn't just sex, he genuinely loved me. I'm surprised you weren't aware of it, Charles.'

'I didn't notice him coming on to you more than he did to anyone else.'

'Then you must have had your eyes shut for the entire period. Everyone else in the cast saw what was happening. God, if I wanted to bring a case for sexual harassment against Damian Grantchester, I'd have witnesses coming out of my ears. Not that I'd dream of doing anything of the kind . . . though I am represented by some of the best lawyers in the world. And Hollywood is notorious for the Rottweiler tendencies of its lawyers, as I'm sure you know. No, so far as Damian's concerned, let the old queen live out his days peacefully in his care home in Dorking. I don't have a vindictive nature.

'Anyway, all of this harassment led eventually to a blazing row. I told Damian, in no uncertain terms, to keep his bloody hands to himself. Which he did, though he went into a monumental sulk over the whole business.

'Charles, you've heard the old chestnut about revenge being a dish best served cold. Damian Grantchester has had a good few years to let his resentment cool down, but now he's decided that his dish of revenge is also going to be a dish of dirt. His motivation is just the spite of a rejected lover. I'm surprised you even thought his accusations worth repeating to me.'

'Well, I . . .'

Justin picked up the spy camera from the table, and handed it across. 'I suggest you take this little gizmo, go back to your dressing room, and prepare for this evening's performance with your customary half-bottle of Bell's.'

Charles couldn't help saying, 'I'm actually off the Bell's.'

'I'm glad to hear it. Not before time.'

That was patronizing again, and Charles wasn't ready to leave just yet. 'I'm afraid there are still more questions I want to ask about the spy camera.'

'Well, don't bloody ask me about it!' It was the first time during their conversation that Justin had lost his cool. 'If you're really interested in who was spying on Liddy Max, then you're talking to the wrong man.'

'So, who should I be talking to?'

'Someone who loved her. More than loved, was obsessed by her. Someone who was so jealous, he was quite capable of arranging to have a spy camera set up in her dressing room. And quite capable of killing her if he saw her with another man!'

'Are you talking about her husband, Derek?'

'I didn't know she even had a husband.'

'Then who are you talking about?'

'God, you're unobservant, Charles. Didn't you notice him, right through the rehearsal period, his eyes following her every movement like a devoted puppy?'

'Who?'

'Seamus Milligan.'

TWENTY

It was a very abstracted Brother Benedict who walked his way through *The Habit of Faith* that Saturday night. He'd checked with Kell, who said she wasn't expecting Seamus Milligan to be in that evening. He was there quite often, kept a close eye on the show. Or maybe he just revelled in seeing his name outside a West End theatre. Kell said Seamus had talked of coming to see it again one day the following week.

Charles could have phoned the writer from his dressing room – the mobile number was on the company contact sheet – but he didn't want to rush into a confrontation. Apart from anything else, Charles wanted time to assess his recent conversation with Justin. Although the star had dealt very fluently with the potential accusations, Charles was not a hundred per cent convinced of his innocence. For the time being, until he'd thought the situation through, he gave equal weight to Damian Grantchester's testimony.

Then there was the business of Seamus Milligan's eyes following Liddy Max's every movement 'like a devoted puppy'. Charles knew he could sometimes be unobservant, but his antennae for the complex business of attraction and counter-attraction in a rehearsal room were usually pretty acute.

And the setting up of the spy camera . . . He still felt certain Gideon had done that. He remembered Baz's words about his friend doing 'little jobs', cash in hand, for 'people' at the Duke of Kent's. Justin Grover had known the stage doorman well from a previous occasion when he'd worked there. Gideon would have liked the idea of doing a secret 'little job' for an international star, particularly if there was money involved.

Whereas, Seamus Milligan . . . Charles had never seen the writer even acknowledge Gideon. The idea of the two of them being complicit in setting up the spy camera didn't feel right.

And Justin's talk of being 'represented by some of the best lawyers in the world' and their 'Rottweiler tendencies' . . . well, the more he thought about it, the more he identified it as a subtle form of bullying. You mess with me and you'll regret it.

No, Charles Paris was far from convinced that all the mysteries surrounding Liddy Max's death had been solved.

He was still troubled and preoccupied when he left the Duke of Kent's that evening. By chance, Grant Yeoell was only a few paces ahead of him. As Charles emerged from the stage door, he heard the tall actor call out, 'Night, night, Shell', before setting off for whatever excitements the night ahead promised him.

Shell. Shelley. Charles recalled an earlier conversation with Grant Yeoell, when the actor had criticized him for referring to his fans as 'groupies'. He had then spoken of one fan who turned up every night for the entire run of a West End show he was in. She'd been called Shelley. Was it possible . . .?

He felt an idiot for not having thought of her before. He'd been conscious of the girls outside the stage door every night, but never looked closely at them. Never thought of them as potential witnesses.

The girl was looking disconsolately in the direction that the now invisible Grant Yeoell had taken, as Charles approached her. 'Big fan of his, are you?'

'His Number One Fan,' she asserted. Her voice was very young, with a London twang.

'Want to talk to me about him?'

Shelley stepped into the light and looked Charles up and down. She was a slight figure, with huge dark eyes set in a very thin face, which was framed by the fur hood of a parka. 'All right,' she said.

The pub, the one he'd been to with Gideon, had now been brightened up with some premature Christmas lights. The bar was Saturday night noisy, and it took him a while to get in his drink order. Vodka and Coke for Shelley, sparkling water for him. He was half afraid she'd have slipped away from the cramped corner where he had left her.

But, when he returned, she was still there, resisting the banter of a bunch of rowdy men with football scarves. She took a long sip from her drink as soon as it was handed across. 'Bloody cold out there,' she said.

'Yes,' Charles agreed. 'Do you wait for Grant every night?' She nodded. 'You certainly must be his Number One Fan.'

'He's nice to me.'

'Nice in what way?'

'Always calls me by my name. Called me "Shell" tonight. After he first found out my name, he used to call me "Shelley". Now he knows me better, it's "Shell".'

'When you say he knows you better, how much better does he know you?'

The girl looked puzzled. A wrinkle appeared between the brows of a face that was otherwise wrinkle-free. 'What do you mean?'

'Has Grant ever taken you out?'

'Of course not.' She giggled at the absurdity of the idea.

'Have you ever had a long conversation with him?'

'He chatted quite a bit when he first signed my programme.'

Charles noticed she was still carrying one, crumpled and a bit wrinkled where the damp had got to it. There must have been rain on some of the nights she maintained her vigil outside the stage door.

'And have you had any long chats with him since?'

'Sometimes he says a few words.' She looked earnestly at Charles. 'I do love him, you know.'

'I'm sure you do.'

'I think he's realizing that, slowly. You know, in time I'm sure he'll come round to the idea. I bet I've watched his movies more times than anyone else does.'

'You probably have. And have you got a boyfriend?'

'No. Just Grant. It is true love, you know, Grant and me. He will realize it some time. He'll marry me in the end.'

'Right.' Charles cleared his throat, and couldn't help himself from saying something terribly old-fashioned. 'What do your parents think about you being out in the West End every night?'

'I don't see my parents. I was in care for a long time.'

'And now?'

'I manage.' But the 'woman of the world' air with which she tried to carry this off didn't quite work. Charles looked at her more closely. Under all that make-up, she really was very young. Fifteen, possibly only fourteen. He remembered Justin and Grant's banter about checking passports.

'And when did you first come to the Duke of Kent's; you know, how soon after *The Habit of Faith* opened?'

'I was here from the start.'

'The Press Night?'

'I don't know what you mean. First night I came was the day you started rehearsing here.'

'The Monday?'

'Yes.'

'How did you know we were rehearsing here?'

'Got a friend who works up the West End. She saw some people going in the stage door. Including Grant. She told me to get round there as soon as I could.'

'Is she a fan of his too?'

'Yes, but not, like, not his Number One Fan. I mean, she came, like, for the first few days after the show opened. She hasn't been for weeks now.' The words were spoken with a mixture of contempt and satisfaction.

'Could we go back to that first Monday when you came to the theatre?'

'OK.'

'What time did you arrive?'

'Like, late afternoon. Five o'clock, maybe. I couldn't get here earlier.'

'But we'd stopped rehearsing by then.'

'I know. I was told that.'

'By whom?'

'The fat man by the door.'

'So then did you go home?'

'No. I thought, like, if this is where Grant's working, then he might come back.'

'And did he?'

'Yes. I saw you first. Round quarter-past six, half-past maybe, I was going to give up, but then you went into the theatre and I thought, well, if Charles Paris is going in, maybe they are rehearsing, and Grant will be along in a minute.'

'How did you know my name was Charles Paris?'

'I didn't then.' She tapped the programme. 'But now I know the names of everyone in the cast.'

'Who else did you see go in that night? After me?'

'The girl, Liddy Max, she went in. Then, a little after that, Grant appeared. I was so excited, because I hadn't seen him – like, in the flesh – since the press launch for *Vandals and Visigoths 5: Revenge of the Skelegators*. But he didn't see me that evening. He had his coat collar turned up, and a hat down over his eyes, but I knew it was him. I'd recognize Grant Yeoell anywhere.'

'And did you see him come out of the theatre?'

'Yes. Like, half an hour later, maybe. And I went forward to, like, say hello, but he blanked me. I felt terrible. He's been nicer to me since I've seen him since, but then I felt, like, Oh my God, it's so awful!'

'What happened next? That evening?'

'I went back.'

'Home?'

'Where I'm staying.' She made the distinction clear.

'And you didn't see anything else?' asked Charles, disappointment and frustration welling up inside him.

'No.'

'You didn't see any of the other actors go in through the stage door?'

'None of the actors, no.'

'What do you mean? Somebody else went in?'

'Yes.' Shelley opened her programme and, knowing her way well around its contents, opened the relevant page. She pointed to a photograph. 'He went in.'

It was Seamus Milligan.

'I can't thank you enough,' said Charles.

'Don't thank me.' The girl giggled. 'I haven't done anything yet.'

'What do you mean?' And then he suddenly did realize what she meant.

'There's a room I can use, just round the corner. What it'll cost, of course, depends on what you want.'

'I don't want anything, Shelley.' He reached into his wallet, pulled out a couple of twenties and thrust them into her hands. 'There, you take that.'

And he rushed out of the pub.

Charles couldn't make sense of it, the naiveté of an underage girl who made her living as a prostitute and was sustained by the fantasy that she would end up marrying an international movie star. He tried not to think about Shelley, of how she spent her life, of where she would be going when she left the pub. It was too upsetting.

He was wandering aimlessly. The temptation to have a drink was overpowering. It was only quarter to eleven, nothing to stop him from nipping into one of the many pubs in the West End and downing a quadruple scotch. Nothing to stop him from buying an overpriced bottle of Bell's at one of the West End's many convenience stores and going back to Hereford Road to numb himself quietly at home.

But he resisted the temptation. Though the sessions at Gower House had done nothing yet to cure his addiction, they had adjusted the time-clock of his guilt. Now he felt guilty when contemplating having a drink; previously he'd only felt guilty the morning after having had too many of them. Was that a kind of progress?

Suddenly, standing in front of the Christmas-lit frontage of an electrical store on Old Compton Street, Charles had total recall of what he had seen on the night of Liddy Max's death. The reality was more disappointing than he'd hoped.

He remembered, when he'd woken up in his dressing room, he'd had recollections of actions seen and conversations overheard, but he now knew those were just dreams. He hadn't been in any mysterious fugue state, simply drunk.

And when it returned, the memory of the one part of the evening that had been wiped away turned out to be surprisingly banal. He had woken at a quarter to eleven, panicked about having stood Frances up, grabbed his bottle of Bell's, and rushed out of the dressing room.

But he hadn't gone straight down the two flights of stairs. On the first-floor landing, he had seen Liddy Max's door open, and gone to investigate. The dressing room was empty, but that was when he had seen its interior. That's why he recognized it.

He had then continued down the second flight of stairs and found Liddy's body.

It was nothing, a tiny detail, but it frightened him. If alcohol could erase that memory, it was capable of erasing much more important ones. And erasing recollections of his own actions and behaviour.

Charles couldn't have said whether it was by coincidence or his own volition that he next found himself standing outside the metal door of the Techie's Drinking Club, but it was certainly by his own will that he entered the premises.

The place was full, but not as rammed as the Saturday night pubs, so its members found the place a welcome haven.

And Charles felt it was where he should be, too. After his moment of total recall, he had a strange sensation that the events of the rest of the night were preordained.

So, it was no surprise to him to meet Baz, smellier and more trembly than ever, holding a bottle of vodka, which was easier to manage than a glass.

'Bad news about Gideon,' said Charles.

The little man looked up at him suspiciously through the glaze on his eyes. 'Who are you?'

'Charles Paris.' The name did not register. 'We met before. I'm in the play at the Duke of Kent's.' Still no recognition. 'The one with all those bloody monks maundering on, and Justin Grover poncing around in a cassock.'

Having his own words quoted back to him did spark something in Baz's memory. 'You came with Gid.'

'That's right. I was just saying, bad news about what happened to him.'

'Oh, it was his own fault,' Baz went on in pious tones. 'People who drink too much must accept the consequences.'

'Do you know anything about how he died?'

'He drank too much. He choked on his own vomit. That is why,' said Baz, still mocking, 'on the rare occasions when I have had too much to drink, I am always very careful to go to sleep lying on my side.'

'I found Gideon in here,' said Charles.

'Did you? And were you the one who called the police?'

'No.'

'Somebody did. We only just had time to get the body out on to the street. Otherwise the police would have been all over this place, asking unhelpful questions about licensing and that kind of nonsense.' Baz took a long swig of vodka to restore his equilibrium.

'Did you see Gideon the night he died?'

'"Night he died"?' The eyes had glazed over again. 'When was that?'

'A few weeks back. I reckon Gideon must've come in here out of normal opening hours.'

'Ah. That could be right. He had a key.'

'Did he often come in out of hours?'

'Not often. Sometimes.'

'Ever with you?'

Baz nodded sagaciously, and took another pull on the vodka bottle.

'Recently?'

'I can't remember when. Dates, not very good at dates. Not very good when I went on dates, either. Brewer's droop.' He seemed to find this very funny. His laughter set up a bout of coughing, which he pacified with vodka.

Charles shifted the point of attack. 'Last time you came here out of hours with Gideon, was it just the two of you?'

'Just the two of us.' Baz nodded vigorously.

'And anyone else?'

He nodded again. 'And someone else.'

'Who?'

'A pal. A drinking pal.'

'And did you all leave at the same time?'

'What time?'

'The same time. Did you all leave together?'

Baz pondered this question. 'Out of hours. Did we all leave together?'

'That's it.'

Charles waited, not very hopefully, but then Baz said, in a tone of some bewilderment, 'Gid didn't leave. Gid died.'

'Here?'

'Yes.'

So at least that probably meant they were talking about the right date. Charles persevered. 'Were you here when he died?'

'No, no. He lay on his back. Always sleep on your side.'

'So, when you left, Baz, was Gideon alone?'

'Don't drink alone. Bad thing to drink on your own. Drinking should be a social activity. "Hail, fellow, well met", and that kind of thing. Don't drink alone.'

'But did you leave Gideon on his own?'

'No, no. Drinking companion. I had to go. Pressing appointment, can't remember what. They went, I stayed. No, no. I went, they stayed.'

'Gideon?'

'Yes.'

'And who?'

'Well, the person we came here with.'

Charles tried not to let his exasperation show. 'And who was that?'

Baz raised a quivering finger and pointed across the room. 'He's over there.'

*   *   *

'I thought you were a Guinness man?'

'Needs must when the devil drives. Nothing on draught here. Just bottles.' Seamus Milligan had one of Jameson's in front of him. 'Do you want to fetch a glass, Charles?'

'No, I'm fine, thank you.'

'Good. Nice when we're all fine, isn't it?'

'Kell said you weren't going to be in today.'

'I wasn't in. To the theatre. I'm here.'

'Yes.'

'Anyway, where I am and what I do there, I would have thought is my business.'

'Certainly. So long as Justin approves.'

'And what the hell do you mean by that, Charles?'

'I mean that you and Justin seem to be quite close.'

'If you're insinuating that he and I—'

'I'm certainly not insinuating anything of a sexual nature. More of a mutually backscratching nature. You both have reasons for doing each other favours.'

'What are you talking about?'

'Let's start with one very simple question, Seamus. Would *The Habit of Faith* be currently running in the West End if Justin Grover wasn't involved in it?'

'Quite possibly. It's a play which I'm very proud of, and I'm sure with another actor . . .' The playwright wasn't even convincing himself.

'No. "With another actor", it might get a few weeks at some regional theatre, a brief tour, but West End? No. You know that as well as I do, Seamus. But with Justin Grover's name attached, a West End run is guaranteed. A reading of the Yellow Pages with Justin Grover's name attached would get a West End run.

'So why, when Justin sees a break coming in his *Vandals and Visigoths* schedule, a break into which he could fit three months in the West End, why doesn't he go for a classic play, or a new one by one of the vibrant young playwrights who keep being discovered? Why does he go for *The Habit of Faith*? It has to be because he owes you a favour.'

'Justin has admired my work for a long—'

'Or, of course, because Justin knows that you could do him a disfavour.'

'Meaning what exactly?'

'Meaning that you know something from his past, something which might rather discredit his image in these hypersensitive times. Something like the fact that Justin Grover enjoys a little voyeurism.'

The expression on the playwright's face told Charles that he was on the right track, and emboldened him to go on assembling his theory out loud. 'Some years back, you were down at Bridport, being shown round the theatre by Damian Grantchester, because one of your plays was in rehearsal there. The previous production had been *Hamlet*, in which Justin and I had given our Rosencrantz and Guildenstern – or possibly the other way round. You were with Damian when he was shown the hole that Justin had drilled through from our dressing room into Ophelia's. You saw the evidence that Justin Grover was a Peeping Tom.'

Seamus's face still gave Charles no discouragement from continuing, 'Well, you sat on that information for a long time, didn't you? I'm not sure why you suddenly decided the moment was right to use it. Was it the change in the world of showbiz, the new climate in which big names were being exposed for long-ago "inappropriate behaviour"? Was it the ever-increasing international profile of Justin Grover? Or was it some decline in your own personal circumstances that meant you needed the money? I don't know, and the details aren't really important. But the outcome was that *The Habit of Faith*, written by Seamus Milligan, appeared in the West End, starring Justin Grover.'

There was a silence. Then the playwright said, 'You have no proof of any of this.'

'No? Maybe not. But that's the history. Let's move up to the present, shall we? What about the death of Liddy Max? Shall we talk about that now?'

The boisterous noise-level around them should have made conversation difficult, but in the two men's cocoon of concentration they might have been alone in the room.

'And what about Gideon's? Let's deal with Liddy first. Shall I tell you what Justin's version of events is?'

'Why not?'

'He's fingering you as her murderer.'

'What?'

'He said you pushed her down the stairs backstage at the Duke of Kent's.'

'Why would I do that?'

'According to Justin, because you were in love with her.'

'What!' That was clearly not the answer Seamus had been expecting.

'Yes. You'd had your eyes on her right through rehearsal, apparently. And when you saw her making love with another man, you flipped your lid and killed her.'

'Is that what Justin said?'

'Yes.'

'And did he say how I happened to see Liddy and Grant making love?'

'No, he didn't,' said Charles, salting away the useful nugget of information that Seamus knew the identity of the girl's lover.

'I'll tell you how it happened, Charles. That Monday evening, I went round to Justin's hotel room, by arrangement. I knocked on the door, got no response and went in. The reason he hadn't heard my knock was that Justin was in a . . . state of some excitement, watching a live transmission on his laptop of Liddy and Grant having sex!'

'So he was lying when he told me you loved her?'

'Absolutely. I've never had any interest in Liddy. Apart from anything else, I'm still a Catholic, so far as marriage is concerned. I may no longer be faithful to the Church, but I have been faithful to my wife since the day of our wedding!'

'So,' asked Charles, 'if it wasn't the passion of a jealous lover, what was the reason you killed Liddy Max?'

'I didn't go near the Duke of Kent's after lunchtime that day.'

'Oh, you did. A witness saw you entering the stage door some half-hour after Grant left the theatre.' There was no response. 'Shall I suggest something that *might* have happened, Seamus?'

'I can't stop you.'

'I think Justin told you to do it. I think Liddy had somehow found out about the secret filming and had called him, probably while you were still in his hotel room. A call was definitely made from her mobile after Grant had left. She threatened to expose Justin to the press. He couldn't risk that, so he sent you round to deal with her.'

'And why would I do that? According to your analysis of my motivation, all I wanted to do was get *The Habit of Faith* into the West End. I'd achieved that. Why would I agree to do a favour for Justin?'

This was not a question for which Charles had been prepared, but he quickly improvised a response. 'I think he was holding out some other offer for you. A nice writing berth on *Vandals and Visigoths*, maybe? I'm sure he has the power to recommend new writers to the producers. The money you'd get for that kind of screenplay would come in handy, wouldn't it? Nice pension for a writer your age.'

The playwright said nothing, but something in his eyes told Charles he was very close to the truth.

'So, Seamus, shall we move on to Gideon's death? Again, I think you did that under orders from Justin. Gideon was a loose cannon, particularly when he'd got a few drinks inside him. Maybe he even threatened to tell the police about Justin paying him to set up the spy camera. He was a risk, anyway, and also a very easy person to kill. Given his weight, given his general state of health, given his alcohol habit . . . someone just had to sit with him for long enough, ply him with vodka for long enough; see that, when he passed out, he was lying on his back . . . and let nature take its course . . .'

'And you think I did that, Charles?'

'Yes. Right here. In this very room.'

'Nonsense!'

'What's more, I have a witness.'

'Who?'

Charles pointed across to where his witness, overcome by excess, lay crumpled on the floor.

'Baz?' said Seamus contemptuously. 'Who's going to believe someone like him?' Then he turned back to Charles and said, 'Well, I feel congratulations are due. You've got a lot of things right. I did cause the deaths – I'm not going to say "murdered" – of both Liddy Max and Gideon. And do you know why I have no anxiety about telling you that, Charles?

'It's because I know for an absolute fact that you haven't a hope in hell of proving any of it.'

TWENTY-ONE

The infuriating thing was that Seamus Milligan's words turned out to be true.

Charles Paris knew exactly what had happened. Seamus had admitted that he was right, and yet the only proof he could put forward depended on the testimony of a street-dwelling alcoholic prone to memory lapses, and an underage prostitute. If Charles had had the full power of the police force behind him, the Crown Prosecution Service would still never have taken to court a case based on such flimsy evidence.

So, all he could do, for the remainder of *The Habit of Faith*'s run, was to continue to work with a man whom he knew to be a Peeping Tom. And whom he knew to have ordered the killing of two people.

To call the situation frustrating would have been an understatement.

And having to act with Justin Grover every night, particularly in the role of Brother Benedict, The Monk Who Just Listened To All Of The Other Monks Who Maundered On In Long Speeches About Their Own Internal Conflicts, did not improve Charles's mood.

Adding to his woes – and, incidentally removing another link in his frail chain of investigative logic – Charles discovered from an obituary in *The Times* that Damian Grantchester had died. He would not have thought any more about it, had he not met Trevor Race again on his next visit to Gower House.

'Heard about Damian, did you?'

'Yes. Saw it in *The Times.*'

'Pathetically short obit, wasn't it? Guy like Damian, put his entire life into the theatre, gave their first break to some of our most distinguished actors, and what do we get? "Launched the meteoric career of Justin Grover." There was more about Justin in the obit than there was about Damian. Bloody press – never been able to recognize real talent.'

'No.'

'Anyway, will you be going, Charles?'

'Where?'

'To the funeral.'

'Oh, I thought that would already have happened.'

'No, the bodies stack up this time of year. Running up to Christmas, takes weeks to get a slot. It's on Monday. Eleven a.m. in Dorking.'

'Oh.'

'I'm going. I've got the details. Do you want them?'

'Yes, please,' said Charles, suddenly making up his mind. 'I do want to be there.'

He mentioned the funeral to Justin Grover, and was unsurprised to be told that the star couldn't attend. 'Costume fitting on Monday for the next tranche of *Vandals*. But do give my best wishes to anyone who might appreciate them.'

Tod Singer said he hadn't known Damian Grantchester well enough to be at the funeral. And, as for the other member of *The Habit of Faith* who had a Bridport connection, Seamus Milligan had not been seen around the Duke of Kent's since his encounter with Charles in the Techie's Drinking Club.

The Monday was cold, but still and rather beautiful. Frost outlined the twigs of trees in the Dorking graveyard. And the funeral was that contemporary rarity, a church service followed by a burial.

It wasn't a bad turnout. Damian Grantchester clearly had the knack of making friends, and Charles felt a twinge of guilt at not having seen more of him in recent years. Once again, it was that theatre thing of being very close to people during a production, and forgetting them the moment you stopped working together. Still, there were a few faces Charles recognized, and a few hands waved across the aisle.

Damian had not apparently had a permanent partner, but there were a lot of middle-aged men, who had once been beautiful, snivelling in their pews.

There is always one good thing about theatrical funerals. The eulogies have been worked on like play scripts. Both they and the readings are perfectly delivered. And the hymn-singing isn't bad either.

Charles felt quite a pang when Damian Grantchester's coffin entered its last home.

*   *   *

'You're Charles Paris, aren't you?'

He admitted that he was, but looked without recognition at the dumpy woman who'd approached him. 'I'm sorry. Got a dreadful memory for faces. I'm not sure—'

'Eve Blanche. We worked together at Bridport.'

'Of course we did! Imperial Theatre. Damian's production of *Hamlet*. You were Ophelia.'

'And you were Rosencrantz. Or was it Guildenstern?'

'Can't remember, but I was definitely in it.'

They were in a private room in a pub near the church. The piles of sandwiches were diminishing at a rate of knots. (What is it about actors and food?) There were also tempting rows of glasses filled with red and white wine. Charles felt very virtuous nursing the tap water he'd asked for at the bar.

'Anyway, it's lovely to see you, Eve. Are you still "in the business"?' If she was, she must have moved on from *ingénue* to character parts.

'No. I didn't do much after Bridport, really. I'm not sure if I had the necessary talent.'

'I have great memories of your Ophelia.' Charles hadn't actually been that impressed at the time, but he knew the right thing to say to a fellow artiste.

'Anyway, after a few years of waiting for the phone to ring and agonizing over whether I had any talent or not, I decided to go off in a completely new direction. Went into publishing.'

'Did you? Ah. Are you the person Damian mentioned who was hawking round his memoir?'

'That's me. *Beginners, Please*. It's an uphill struggle. Publishers are so obsessed by celebrity these days. I've hardly got a flicker of interest from anyone – except one publisher who had the nerve to suggest that, because Damian had known him, he should write an unauthorized biography of Justin Grover. He reckoned there was a market for that.'

'How dispiriting.' Then Charles couldn't help asking the inevitable actor's question: 'Is there anything in the memoir about me?'

'You get a mention, yes. There's a lot of very interesting stuff in there.' Her tone had become more purposeful.

'I'm sure there is. I'd love to talk to you in more detail about it, Eve.'

'I'd like that too. Can't really do it here, wouldn't be right on this occasion.'

'No.'

'But maybe after we leave here? I came past a little coffee shop on my way to the church. If you've got time . . .?'

'My next call is "the half" at the Duke of Kent's. I've got time.'

Charles sipped at his black Americano while Eve found the relevant part of *Beginners, Please* on her tablet. She handed it across to him. 'I don't think it was just Damian's lack of celebrity that made all those publishers turn the book down. I think they were worried about the libel risk.'

He read the passage indicated.

Rosencrantz and Guildenstern were played by two young actors who were destined to have very different careers. The first was Charles Paris, an adequate jobbing actor who might have gone on to greater things had he not been so wedded to the bottle.

Ouch! That put him in his place.

But the trajectory of my Guildenstern was destined to be very different. His name was Justin Grover, and he certainly had no more talent than Charles Paris.

A kind of back-handed compliment, maybe . . .?

Justin was one of those annoying actors, who relied completely on technique rather than emotion. Every nuance of his own performance was worked out, though he never considered how it might fit in with what the rest of the company was doing. Someone like that is extremely irritating to direct. There is only one role in the theatre where that kind of approach works, and that is when the person deploying it is a star. Stars can do more or less what they want, and the rest of the company just has to fit in around them.

And – irony of ironies – Justin Grover did actually become a star. How someone of such minimal talent could rise to such heights does not cause me any surprise. I've seen the same thing happen in the theatre too often for it to occasion in me even the mildest flicker of an eyelash. Why it was Justin Grover rather than, say, Charles Paris, on whom the Blind Goddess of Good Fortune smiled, I have no idea. But I do get bloody annoyed with people saying, 'Oh, I gather you gave Justin Grover his first break, you must be proud of that', as if I'd achieved nothing else in my life!

And I guess there are now many thousands – possibly millions – of people across the world who think he is a good actor. He's certainly constantly being quoted in the media. And rumours abound that he might soon join the ranks of our theatrical knights. That talent-free bastard is already halfway to being a National Treasure.

What Justin Grover's success prompts in me is what I always think of as 'The Mozart Question'. It is the one raised in Peter Shaffer's delightfully clever play Amadeus. *If a man creates some of the most beautiful music the world has ever heard, does it matter if in person he is an emotional retard with a lavatorial sense of humour? In other words, does the personal behaviour of an artist have any relevance in the appreciation of their artistry?*

In my view, having spent my life working with people who range from absolute charmers to total shits, I think the answer is yes.

To be more specific, is my appreciation of Justin Grover's achievements coloured by the fact that I know him to be a sleazy voyeur?

Damian Grantchester then went on to chronicle precisely the discovery the maintenance men had made in the Imperial Theatre dressing room which had been shared during his production of *Hamlet* by Charles Paris and Justin Grover. He also presented the corroborating evidence that had been given by Eve Blanche when he questioned her about the incident. She related how Justin Grover had made a teasing reference to a particular mole on the front of her thigh, something which could only have been observed by someone who had seen her naked. Eve had commented to Damian:

'It made me feel unwholesome, defiled somehow. But now you've told me about the peephole, I feel even worse.' And when I saw her some years later, Eve told me, 'Having been the object of a voyeur's attentions had a profound effect on my life. I completely lost confidence in myself, both as a woman and an actress. The experience was the main reason for my

giving up my career in the theatre. I think it's also why I never
got married or was able to sustain a long-term relationship.'
So that's another triumph for Sigismund the Strong!

Charles looked up from the tablet. He had felt Eve's eyes locked on
him during his reading. 'Well?' she said. 'That's proof, isn't it?'

He grimaced. 'It was proof for Damian. It's proof for you. It's
proof for me. But would it stand up in court? Would allegations in
an unpublished memoir stand a chance against someone who, in
his owns words, is "represented by some of the best lawyers in the
world"?' The company behind *Vandals and Visigoths* is a very
major player in the entertainment world. They wouldn't let their
multimillion-dollar franchise be threatened by twenty-year-old accusations about something that happened to a young actress in the
Imperial Theatre, Bridport.'

'Wouldn't they, Charles?'

'What do you mean by that?'

'Times have changed. The whole climate's different now. Twenty-
year-old accusations about "inappropriate behaviour" towards young
actresses are exactly the kind of things that are now being taken
seriously.'

'Yes, I've read all that stuff in the papers. And maybe, if you
could call on Damian's testimony to back you up, you might—'

'I've made a start, Charles.'

'A start on what?'

'I've tracked down the builder who was doing the maintenance
work in the Imperial Theatre. He's retired now, but still very articulate. He's fully prepared to stand up in court and describe how he
found the peephole that was drilled in the dressing-room wall.

'I've got funding from a women's action group, and I've instructed
solicitors.

'I'm going to fight this, Charles. I'm going to fight this all the
way.'

The sequence of events, set in motion by Eve Blanche's deter-
mination, unfolded over many years. But she was right, the climate
of opinion had changed, and it had changed in her favour.

Even twenty years before, she would have been lucky to have
found a solicitor willing to take up her cause. And many people
then might not have considered sexual voyeurism even as a

crime. Not admirable behaviour perhaps, but 'the kind of thing men do'.

Above all, the company behind *Vandals and Visigoths* would have used the considerable muscle of their legal and PR departments to silence Eve Blanche before she even got started on her campaign.

But social media had changed all that. Within hours of Eve's allegations becoming public, they had been forwarded and retweeted many times. More importantly, the publicity led to a lot more women coming forward, saying that they too had suffered from Justin Grover's voyeurism. Some were the usual cranks who leap on to any bandwagon of complaint, but enough of them could produce solid evidence that would make their accusations stick.

One effect of social media, bemoaned by the crustier supporters of the British legal system, had been an erosion of the old principle that everyone is innocent until they have been proved guilty. Long before he had been charged with any crime, Justin Grover's reputation had been smeared. Voyeurism was such a sneaky, unpleasant practice. Despised by those tabloid readers who provide such a groundswell of British public opinion. It had only been a matter of time before the headlines on the lines of 'SIGISMUND THE SLEAZY' and 'SIGISMUND THE SICK' appeared.

The reaction from the producers of *Vandals and Visigoths* was again very different from what it might have been a few decades earlier. Back then, they would have gone straight into Damage Limitation mode, resorting to any means – even criminal – to keep the whitewash on their precious stars unsullied. Now, they regarded their stars as the source of the damage they wished to limit. Again, long before any formal charges had been laid against him, Justin Grover was suspended from further involvement in *Vandals and Visigoths*.

And, only a few months later, an announcement was made to allay the anxieties of the franchise's many international fans. Yes, *Vandals and Visigoths* would be continuing. But future storylines would be built around Wulf, who, following the death in battle of his father, was now the sole bastion of civilization against the ferocious wrath of Spurg and the Skelegators.

So, Grant Yeoell, an actor with a gym-sculpted body, but even less talent than his predecessor (and to Charles Paris's mind, less talent than a plank of wood or a bowl of porridge), was elevated to the status of global star.

Before the decision was made, the producer's legal department made deep investigations into Grant's private life. Their discovery, that he had no permanent partner, but slept with a large number of consenting, adult females, they regarded as rather good news. The publicity department thought they could make a lot of that.

So, Grant Yeoell continued serenely on his route to the top, enjoying the favours of as many women as he wanted to. There was nothing illegal about that yet. So long, of course, as he checked their passports first.

Legal processes being slow – as are all processes for which the practitioners are paid by the hour – the outing and vilification of Justin Grover did not begin until long after the run of *The Habit of Faith* had ended.

And Charles Paris never heard whether the subsequent investigations also led to Justin's involvement in the deaths at the Duke of Kent's Theatre being proved.

TWENTY-TWO

C harles never saw Baz again. Whether the poor man had been found one morning dead in a gutter, or somehow survived, there was no way of knowing. Though Charles thought the former scenario was the more likely.

Another event, of which Charles would be completely unaware, was the marriage, less than a year after his wife's death, of Derek Litwood. His bride was a trainee solicitor in the same legal firm, a girl whose ambitions did not extend beyond raising a family in Muswell Hill and supporting her husband at professional functions. No inappropriate ambitions there.

The only other thing that happened before *The Habit of Faith* run ended was that Tod Singer and Kell Drummond, both now staunch devotees of Alcoholics Anonymous, announced their engagement.

That resonated with Charles, because the only area of his life that brought him any satisfaction at that time was the progress he was making at Gower House. Three days a week without alcohol moved on to four, then five. And three weeks before the end of *The Habit of Faith* run, he achieved a full week without any booze passing his lips. He couldn't define how it was working, but something inside his brain was changing. The only thing he knew for certain was that he did get a weekly charge from telling his fellow participants about his days of abstinence.

Passing a day without alcohol, though, did not now seem so incongruous, so alien. He even on occasion managed to go to a pub with alcohol-drinking friends and survive on sparkling water.

He didn't want to make any generalizations or predictions about his progress. The urge to have a drink, prompted by an advertisement on the tube, or someone on television picking up a large Scotch, could still be agonizing. He could never imagine it going away completely. He also knew that one reckless drinking session could destroy everything he had worked so hard to achieve.

And he was worried about how he'd manage when the run of *The Habit of Faith* ended. Because his minimal experience of not drinking when he was out of work was that the evenings did seem inordinately long. And when he didn't drink, he watched more television. Drinking meant going out with people, not drinking meant sitting at home alone.

There wasn't much television he enjoyed, particularly not the drama. Actors always say how fervently they admire other actors working on television, but it's almost never true. They are so much more professional viewers than the general public, who watch and boost ratings without ever sparing a second to question how the various effects are achieved. Actors are always aware of their fellow actors' little tricks, the artifice with which they perfect tiny, subtle techniques in front of the camera. They also know too much of what goes on in rehearsal rooms, about the horse-trading with directors to achieve another close-up, about how certain star actors see to it that the camera does not linger too long on members of the supporting cast. It's always a bad sign when the star of a long-running series gets a credit as director. That means more close-ups.

Above all, actors watching television are always thinking: Why does that talent-free bastard land this extraordinarily well-paid job when I'd do it much better?

Charles's progress on giving up the booze had not gone unremarked by Frances. Indeed, he had not allowed it to go unremarked. He reported to her assiduously after each 'Growing Out' session. And, a week before *The Habit of Faith* closed, he was able to announce that, come the final Saturday performance, he would have achieved four full weeks without alcohol.

Frances, having known Charles for so long, was aware of the scale of this achievement, and was duly appreciative. 'You haven't got any commitments on the Sunday, have you? The day after the show finishes?'

'I haven't got any commitments for the rest of my life.' It was true. He'd known for long enough when he would next be out of work. He'd vaguely heard other members of the company talking about jobs they'd be going on to, or the inefficiency of their agents in not finding them other jobs to go on to. Charles should really have been on to Maurice Skellern, to encourage him to look out for something else for his client. But Charles had done nothing, secure in the cocoon of three-months' guaranteed West End money. And, of course, he had had other preoccupations.

'Well, let's have lunch then. On the Sunday,' said Frances. 'I'll pick you up in the car.'

'That's very generous of you.'

'I thought you might want to bring some stuff – clothes, shaving kit – over to my place.'

'What, you mean I can stay?'

She backtracked quickly. 'I'm not talking about staying forever. Couple of nights, perhaps? See how we go.'

'Yes. No rush.' But Charles was rather ecstatic at what he was hearing.

'I'll cook a nice lunch.'

'Great.' Then he saw a potential pitfall. 'You haven't invited Juliet and Miles too, have you?

'No, Charles.' Frances chuckled. 'It'll be lunch for just the two of us.'

He smiled. Those encoded words, surviving from early in their marriage, both recognized to mean that they would spend the afternoon in bed.

'And, Charles . . .' said Frances.

'Yes?'

'I'm very proud of you for what you've done. You know, over the booze.'

'Oh. Thank you, Frances.'

So maybe that's how it'll work, thought Charles, as he put the phone down. Although the plans had been unspoken, both envisaged that over the next few weeks Charles would gradually start to spend more time at Frances's place – and in her new place if the purchase worked out – until the moment came when he finally gave up the lease on his studio flat. And husband and wife would once again cohabit.

For Charles, it would be his first positive achievement for many years.

When the curtain came down on *The Habit of Faith* for the last time, Charles felt a mixture of emotions. Relief that he'd never again have to nod understandingly as Brother Benedict, The Monk Who Just Listened To All Of The Other Monks Who Maundered On In Long Speeches About Their Own Internal Conflicts.

And frustration, born of the knowledge that the crimes of Justin Grover and Seamus Milligan would forever go unpunished.

He'd been impressed by Eve Blanche, but he didn't really think there was a hope in hell that anything would come out of her campaign. He could not see what lay ahead.

Oh well, thought Charles Paris, as he hung up his monk's habit for the last time, you win some, you lose some.

There was no official celebration of the last night. The producers had hosted a lavish Company Dinner after the Thursday performance. Nita Glaze had been there, bubbling with confidence about her new West End production.

Charles had got through the dinner without drinking, a considerable achievement in such convivial circumstances.

But after the final show, there was a move, for those of the company who fancied it, to go to the pub 'for a quick one'. Charles thought it would be churlish not to join them. Whatever antagonisms had been felt during the run, now was the time to relax and say what fun it had all been. That was not difficult for anyone, secure in the knowledge that the next day they wouldn't have to see any of the others . . . possibly ever again.

Charles felt secure. He had conquered the booze. Tomorrow would be the start of the final rapprochement between him and Frances.

And then a little tingle of alarm started to sound in his brain. Commitment. He was about to commit himself. Irrevocably.

'What are you drinking, Charles?'

The voice belonged to Imogen Whittaker. Her red hair glistened in the Christmas lights. She looked stunning. In that moment, she represented every beautiful woman the world still had to offer.

In answer to her offer, Charles Paris replied, 'A large Bell's, please.'